For a long while the lad lay half stunned, unconscious. Presently he opened his eyes to look full upon a ghastly spectacle. The lion was devouring the man, mauling what had been its cruel taskmaster and most hated enemy.

Now the lad saw his four-footed friend in a new light. Yesterday he had been but a softly purring kitten. To-day he was a man-eater, rumbling and snarling over a bloody feast—and he and the lad were alone.

As the boy looked up the lion ceased feeding for a moment and raised his head, eyes blazing straight into those of the youth. Then he purred gently and moved his great form to half uncover his victim. His expression and his action constituted an invitation which the boy could not mistake—he had been bidden to the feast!

EDGAR RICE BURROUGHS

Edgar Rice Burroughs is one of the world's most popular authors. With no previous experience as an author, he wrote and sold his first novel, *A Princess of Mars,* in 1912. In the ensuing thirty-eight years until his death in 1950, Burroughs wrote 91 books and a host of short stories and articles. His prolific pen ranged from the American West to primitive Africa and on to romantic adventure on the moon, the planets, and even beyond the farthest star.

No one knows how many copies of ERB books have been published throughout the world. It is conservative to say, however, that of the translations into 32 known languages, including Braille, the number must run into the hundreds of millions. When one considers the additional world-wide following of the TARZAN newspaper feature, radio programs, comic magazines, motion pictures and television, Burroughs must have been known and loved by literally a thousand million or more.

Attesting to the unparalleled holding power Edgar Rice Burroughs maintains upon his readers are the many ERB fan clubs existing today. Established by dedicated Burroughs admirers, some of these groups publish their own fan magazines devoted exclusively to all facets of the Burroughs legend.

Interested admirers of Mr. Burroughs' literary works are cordially invited to write to these fan clubs for information.

TBN (THE BURROUGHS NEWSBEAT),
5813 York Avenue South
Edina, Minnesota 55410
ERBANIA, 8001 Fernview Lane, Tampa, Florida 33615

EDGAR RICE
BURROUGHS
THE LAD AND THE LION

SF

ace books

A Division of Charter Communications Inc.
A GROSSET & DUNLAP COMPANY
51 Madison Avenue
New York, New York 10010

THE LAD AND THE LION

© 1917 Frank A. Munsey Co.

An Ace Book
by arrangement with Edgar Rice Burroughs, Inc.

Printed in U.S.A.

ONE

A stately pile of ancient masonry rose in a great park of linden trees and ash and oak. There were broad, formal and great expanses of level sward. There were sad-faced gleaming marble fountains throwing their shimmering waters into the warm sunlight. There were men in uniform standing guard—tall, splendid fellows. A sad-faced old man walked along neat gravelled pathways through the gardens, past the marble fountains. He was a very erect old man whose unbending shoulders and firm gait belied his age, for he was really a very old man. At the old man's side walked a little boy; and when the two approached them, the soldiers snapped their burnished pieces smartly in salute.

The old man was inordinately proud of the little boy. That was why he liked to have him walk with him in the gardens and down near the great gates where people often gathered to see them as they passed. He liked to have him ride with him through the city in one of the royal carriages where all the people might see him; for when the old man died, the little boy would be king.

"The people seem to like us," said the boy, as they passed the gates and the crowd waved and smiled and cheered. "That is why I cannot understand why they killed my father."

"They do not all like us, said the old man.

"Why don't they?" asked the boy.

"It is not so much that they do not like us as that they do not like kings. They believe that they, who know nothing about ruling, can rule better than we who are trained to rule and whose families have ruled for centuries."

"Well," said the boy, with finality, "they like you; and when I am king, I shall try to rule as you have."

"I could wish that you might never be king," said the old man, bitterly. "It is a thankless job, Michael."

Three men sat on the verandah of a hunting lodge in the cool woods a few miles from the capital. One was a little, myopic man with horn-rimmed spectacles and thin, disordered hair that had not known shears for many weeks. His collar was soiled; so was his shirt, but most of that which showed in the V of his coat collar was hidden by a Windsor tie. He was a mussy little man with mussy clothes and trousers which made him appear about to jump, when he stood. His mind, however, was not mussy. Its facts were well ordered and easily accessible to a glib tongue which could marshal them in any formation that seemed best adapted to the occasion; on it, all facts seemed plastic, assuming any guise the little man desired to give them. Often the little facts' own mothers would not have recognized them.

The other two men were in easy tweeds; loose, comfortable clothes that did not, however, look as though they had been cut to fit someone else, or no one, as did the little man's; also, they were well barbered, and their linen was clean—and linen.

"Your highness will understand," said the little man, "that in the event of an accident which removed the king and Prince Michael we are to have a new constitution, a far more liberal constitution, and that the representatives of the people shall have the deciding voice in government."

The older of the other two nodded. "I understand, Meyer," he said.

"And agree?"

"Certainly. I presume you will be chancellor when I am king?"

"That is understood," said Meyer. "My associates, who collaborated with me in drawing up the new constitution, would insist upon it."

"So the constitution is already drawn," said the younger man, a little testily. "Would it not be well to let his highness see and approve it?"

"That will not be necessary," said Meyer.

"Why?" demanded the younger man.

"Because my associates would not brook any changes in this document into which they have put their best efforts," replied Meyer, suavely.

"Rubbish!" exclaimed the young man. "Why don't you come right out and say the king will be nothing but a figurehead—that you will, in reality, be king?"

"At least, the new king will be alive," said Meyer.

"Come, come, Paul!" said the older man. "I am sure that everything that Meyer and his associates contemplate is in the best interests of the people and the country."

"Absolutely," assured Meyer.

"And we should interpose no obstacles," added H.R.H. Prince Otto.

The young Count Sarnya sniffed.

"We are peculiarly fortunate in being able to eliminate obstacles *permanently*," said Meyer, looking at Sarnya through the thick lenses of his glasses; "and now that everything is understood, I must be going. You know how to reach me if you think it necessary. I—always—know —how—to—reach—you. Good day, your highness; good day, Count Sarnya."

The older man nodded; the young man merely turned his back and walked toward the sideboard, where he poured himself a stiff drink. As the door closed behind Meyer, he gulped it down. "I want to get a bad taste out of my mouth," he snapped; then he wheeled suddenly on the older man. "I thought you told me that it was to be only the old man; you were to be regent if anything happened to him. I didn't know you were going to murder the boy, too."

"Stop!" commanded Otto. "You are overwrought; you don't know what you're saying. I am going to murder no one—that is a nasty word. You know I have had nothing to do with this. They are going to do what they are going to do. No one can stop them. Can I help it if they have offered to make me king? What would have happened had I refused? They'd kill me, too; and Meyer would be dictator. I have had to do it to save the life of my dynasty for my country and my people!"

"Don't get heroic, Otto," said Sarnya. "I think I'll take another drink—I need another."

The morning sun was pouring through the east windows of the palace, presaging a perfect day, as Count Jagst entered the room in answer to the king's summons.

"Look at this, Jagst," said the old king, passing a paper to his chief of staff. "I found it on the floor just under the corridor door as I came in from my quarters."

General Count Jagst took the paper and opened it—a single sheet of note paper on which was typed: "For God's sake, Your Majesty, don't ride out today."

"Who's officer of the guard today?" asked the king. "Someone must have seen who slipped that paper under the door."

"I don't know," said Jagst. "I'll find out." He touched a button, and when a secretary came in response he told him to summon the officer of the guard.

"They're closing in on us, Jagst," said the king. "I don't

8

care for myself—I'm old and tired—but Michael; he's such a little fellow to shoulder all this—and the intrigue and the constant danger to his life. Otto will be regent. That will be bad for the country. Otto never had good sense, and into the bargain he's a damned traitor. If he hadn't been my brother I'd have had him shot years ago —he has deserved it; always plotting against me, working with all my enemies. If anything happens to me, Jagst, take Michael out of the country until things quiet down. If he's needed and wanted, bring him back. That's what the poor little devil will have to pay for being born in line of succession to a throne. The best I can wish for him is that they won't want him. Take him out of Europe, Jagst; and don't let anyone know where you are taking him. They got his father; and if they ever get me, they'll go after him next."

There was a knock on the door. The king nodded to Jagst.

"Come in!" said the chief of staff.

Captain Count Sarnya entered and saluted. "You sent for me, Sir?" He stood very erect, looking the king straight in the eyes.

"Yes, Sarnya," said the monarch. "I found a note that had been slipped under the corridor door, when I came in just now. How could that have happened without someone seeing it done?"

"I have no idea, Sir."

"There is a sentry on duty in the corridor, isn't there?"

"Yes, Sir."

"Make a thorough investigation, Sarnya; and report to me personally. That is all."

As Sarnya closed the corridor door after him, there came a knock on the door that led to the king's apartments; then it flew open before anyone could say, "Come in," or "Stay out." Prince Michael burst in, flushed and eager; but when he saw that the king was not alone, he stopped, stood up very straight, and saluted his grandfather.

The old man looked at the boy and smiled. "Why all the excitement?" he asked.

"We're late," said Michael. "It is past time for our ride—you know you said we would ride in the park today. I particularly like that ride."

"Why do you like it so much?" asked the king.

"Because in the park I see so many little children playing," explained the boy. "I see them sailing their boats on the pond and flying kites and playing games. I should like to sail a boat on the pond in the park. I should also like very much to fly a kite, but one cannot fly a kite in the palace gardens on account of the trees. Then the palace shuts off the wind, too. However, it is nice to watch them flying theirs in the park. I am all ready to go, Grandpa."

"Come here," said the king. He put his hand on the boy's shoulders. "I am going to disappoint you today, Michael," he said. "I am not going to take you with me."

The eagerness went out of the boy's eyes; and his chin trembled a little, but he said, "Yes, Sir," without a tremor in his voice.

"It is also a disappointment to me," said the king, "but something tells me that I have a very important engagement today."

"Yes, Sir," said the boy; "but we shall go again another day, shan't we?"

Then the old king did that which he had never before done in the presence of others. He drew the boy close to him and kissed him.

"I should hate to think that we never should," he said.

"Now run along, my son, and do the best you can in the palace gardens."

As the door closed behind the boy, Jagst turned upon the king. "You don't mean to say that you are going to ride out in the city today, do you?" he demanded fiercely. He even forgot to put in a "Sir" or a "Majesty."

"You wouldn't want them to think that I am afraid of them, would you, Jagst?" demanded the king, a half smile upon his lips.

"I don't give a damn what that scum thinks, Sir," shouted the old general. "I'm only thinking of you, and you should be thinking of your country and your people."

"I am only thinking that I am a king," said the old man, wearily; "and that kings must do what kings are expected to do. My God, Jagst! All my life I have been doing all the things I didn't want to do and none of the things I wanted to do."

"But just today, Sir," pleaded Jagst. "You will not go today?"

"What is the difference, Jagst? If it is not today, it will be tomorrow. Come, walk as far as the carriage with me."

* * * *

"This," said the little Prince Michael to the gardener's son, "would be a very nice boat if it didn't tip over every time we put it in the water. I think there must be something wrong with it. The boats that the children sail in the park do not tip over like this. Have you ever been to the park and seen them sailing their boats?"

"Oh, yes," replied the gardener's son. "I have sailed boats there myself. The trouble with this boat is that it has no keel. It should have a weighted keel; then it wouldn't tip over so easily."

"You have been to the park and sailed a boat?" said the prince, wistfully." I was going there today with my

11

grandfather; but he had a very important engagement, and could not take me with him. Perhaps we shall go tomorrow. What was that?"

"It sounded like one of the big guns at the fort," said the gardener's son.

* * * *

There was rioting in the city that night; and an angry, sullen crowd milled about the great gates before the palace. There were barricades in the streets and machine guns and soldiers and disheveled, loud-mouthed men making speeches.

In the palace a red-eyed boy faced General Count Jagst. "But I do not wish to run away," he said. "My grandfather did not run away."

"It was his wish, Your Majesty," said Jagst. "It was his last command to me."

"Very well, then, Jagst; I am ready."

Servants carried their portmanteaus to a postern door where waited one of the royal motors that the old king had so scorned. As they entered and drove away, a man watching them from a balcony sighed with relief and turned back into the palace. It was Captain Count Sarnya, Officer of the Guard.

TWO

The first intimation that the boy had of the disaster was the consciousness of being roughly awakened in the dead of the night—by what he knew not. The ship still trembled from the shock of the collision; but the noise of the impact had been lost to him in the depths of his deep, childish slumber.

As he rose upon one elbow in his berth he became aware of a great commotion about the steamer, and presently he heard the hoarse voices of the stewards as they called at the doorways of the staterooms, summoning the passengers on deck.

A moment later old Jagst burst into the room where the boy was already getting into his clothes.

"Quick, Your Majesty!" cried the old man. "Come on deck—there is not time to bother about clothes," and he grasped the boy by the arm to drag him from the stateroom.

"No, Jagst," exclaimed the boy, holding back. "Go yourself naked if you will, but for my part I prefer to be properly clothed," and notwithstanding the pleas and urgings of his companion the youth proceeded to don all his apparel before ever he would step his foot from the room.

When they reached the deck they found the utmost confusion reigning. Two boats filled with women and children already had gotten safely away; but now the steerage passengers, crazed with the panic of fear, had rushed upon the remaining boats where the officers and crew were making futile efforts to drive them back.

Women were alternately praying and screaming. Men ran hither and thither in futile search for boats into which they could place their loved ones. Jagst put a strong arm about the boy and pushed him through the fighting mob surrounding one of the boats.

"A child!" he cried to one of the officers. "Have you room for another child?" The old man knew that it was useless then to plead the cause of royal blood—for that night upon the stricken ship, with death reaching out to claim them all, men were stripped to the bone of their primitive brutality. As in the days of creation a man took only that precedence which his courage and brawn entitled him to.

The crew and the officers at this boat had succeeded in driving back the fear-mad mob, and some semblance of order had been restored there. At Jagst's question the officer took the boy by the shoulder and hustled him through the guard of seamen toward the boat, into which women and children were being hurried.

At the ship's side the boy glanced hurriedly about him. On either hand, held back before the revolvers of the crew, were women and children of the steerage. As he saw them his head went up and his young eyes blazed. He turned savagely upon the officer.

"Do you think," he cried, "that I will enter a boat while there are women still on board the ship?" and with that he turned quickly back into the crowd.

The sailors and some of the men passengers gave a little shout of admiration. A woman was called to take the boy's place in the boat. Someone strapped a life belt about the boy's body. The ship was listing terribly to starboard now. The seas were running frightfully high. The noise of the hurricane was deafening, and the lowering clouds that shut out the moon and the stars kept the whole scene enveloped in darkness.

A huge wave struck the ship full upon her port side. Without an instant's warning she rolled over and went down. The boy, with hundreds of others, had been thrown clear of the tangling wreckage of the decks. He found himself amidst a struggling mass of shrieking humanity. The life belt kept his head above water except when a great wave broke over him. The screaming of those about him, especially of the women, affected him much more than did his own danger; but almost immediately the cries lessened, and after each great wave had passed their numbers were gruesomely less.

The boy shuddered. In reality he was but a child—scarce fourteen. Presently a heavy piece of wreckage swept down upon him. In the blackness of the night he did not see it, and as it struck a glancing blow against his skull he lost consciousness.

When his eyes opened again to comprehension of the things about him he discovered that the world was all water and he its sole inhabitant. Buoyed up by the life belt, his nose and mouth were still above the surface of the watery universe. He looked about. Ah, what was that strange thing behind him? It loomed large against the skyline as it rose to the crest of the now diminishing sea, and then it vanished into a deep hole for a moment only to reappear once more.

Presently it came close enough for the boy to reach up and grasp its side—it was one of the boats of the lost steamer. Seizing the gunwale he drew himself up and peered over the edge. Ah, this seemed to offer far greater comforts than the cold, wet, undulating element in which creation had discovered him. He climbed in. For an hour he sat shivering upon a thwart debating the wisdom of leaping back once more into the comparatively warm water of the ocean. Then the sun broke through the clouds—a hot tropic sun that soon warmed his hands and face.

He was puzzled by the radiance and heat of the remarkable thing that had appeared so suddenly above him. This was truly a world of marvels. First there had been nothing but the bottomless, tossing, wetness that had enveloped him. Then had come the spacious and luxurious contrivance into which he had clambered, and now, wonder of wonders, there had sprung through the greyness of the vast above a warm and grateful light and comfort.

His wet clothing, he noticed, kept the warmth from reaching those portions of his body which it covered—it was evident that the blow had not affected his reasoning faculties. Examination of the odd and useless encumbrances which covered him and kept off the pleasant warmth revealed the fact that they were removable. Soon thereafter the boy's entire body was basking in the hot rays of the sun. Fortunately he had not thrown the garments overboard as he had at first been minded to do, and later in the day he was very glad to cover his nakedness from the terrific heat that beat down upon him; but he did not again don the clothing, merely drawing it over him as a covering and protection from the sun.

Hunger and thirst had only commenced to assert themselves poignantly when a ship loomed large and close at hand. It must have been quite close to him for a long time before he discovered it, for not knowing that there was anything to expect other than those things which he had already perceived he had not looked about the horizon in search of other objects.

A light breeze was blowing which eventually drifted the steamer down upon the small boat. The former was a small craft. From its single funnel no smoke issued, and upon its deck but one human being was visible. He leaned over the partially demolished rail watching the tossing small boat with its lonely occupant, a strange, uncouth figure in rags.

As the two boats approached one another, the boy looked up into the bearded face of a gaunt and sinister-looking old man. When they were about to touch, the latter dropped a rope into the youth's hands; then he leaned far over the rail making odd motions with his fingers and uttering strange, uncanny mouthings.

The boy could not understand. The old man danced up and down, shrieking and yelling like a demon; and all the while he wove his fingers into weird gestures. In the midst of his strange performance a deep moan that was half growl broke from something upon the deck behind him that was hid from the boy's sight. The old man turned at the interruption to shake his fist in the direction of the sound, and shriek and gibber his anger; then he turned back to the boy.

This time he took one end of the rope and fastened it about his waist, pointing to the boy and then to the rope which he had tied about himself, nodding his head and again wiggling his fingers frantically. The boy comprehended. The odd creature wished him to fasten his end of the rope about himself. Quickly he saw the purpose and a moment later had done as the old man wished.

Half dragged by the old man and half scrambling by himself, the youth reached the deck of the steamer. Before he had an opportunity to look about him his rescuer had confronted him with flying digits. After a moment of this he would stand still looking expectantly at the boy's hands, and then up into his face. Then he would repeat the operation. At last he seemed to become furious with rage, for he danced up and down shaking his fists and screaming demoniacally.

At last the youth comprehended what was wanted of him. Just as the old fellow had tied the rope about his own waist as a guide to him to do likewise so now his acts were intended as directions for the boy's further deportment—so thought the youth. Therefore he danced up and down, as did the old man, and shrieked and wiggled his fingers.

But the result of this upon the man was anything but what the boy had expected. Instead of being pleased the old fellow became furious. He leaped at the youth, grasped him by the throat, shook him furiously and then beat him cruelly about the face and head. He only ceased when a sudden paroxysm of epilepsy superinduced by his frantic rage laid him stiff and gasping upon the deck.

The boy, released from the grasp of his tormentor, stood rubbing his bruised face and watching the writhing thing upon the deck planking—the hideous thing that rolled with frothing mouth and upturned eyes. Then there broke upon his ears the same deep, moaning growl that he had heard before he gained the steamer's deck, a noise that sent a little thrill through him.

Turning quickly toward the sound he saw a strange, tawny creature within a cage close behind the cabin. The thing went upon all fours, pacing softly back and forth the length of its prison, with lowered head brushing the bars and gleaming yellow eyes glaring menacingly out upon the two whose disturbance it seemed to resent.

It was a young lion, a year old, or perhaps a trifle more. The boy immediately left the grovelling man and walked toward the cage, attracted by this new and wonderful beast. He knew no fear, for with the blow that he had received upon his head all memory had gone—even that which is supposed to be inherited and which is sometimes called instinct. He did not know that the creature in the cage was a lion, or that the other upon the deck was a man, or that he himself was a boy. He had everything to learn, as though he had but just been born.

He walked quite close to the cage. The lion stopped his restless pacing. The boy put his hand through the bars to touch the peculiar creature. Instinctively the great teeth were bared and the beast shrank back from the profaning touch of man, but still further the hand was insinuated into the cage. A puzzled expression expunged the ugly snarl from the young lion's wrinkled face. He stood quite still as the soft hand of the youth touched his soft muzzle. The hand passed back and forth along the head, already showing indications of the massive lines that maturity would bring. Then the lion stepped close to the bars and with half-closed eyes purred contentedly as the boy rubbed and scratched his head and ears. That was the beginning of the strange friendship.

Presently the boy discovered a fragment of raw fish lying just outside the cage where the lion had dropped it during a recent meal. The pangs of hunger quickly asserted themselves at sight of the morsel, and dropping to his haunches the youth seized the unsavory thing and commenced to devour it ravenously, like a starved beast.

While he was thus occupied, the old man recovered from his fit. For a time he sat watching the boy; then he staggered to his feet and went to the galley from which he presently returned with food which he threw upon the deck beside the little waif. The boy looked up gratefully, but the terrible scowl upon the old man's vicious face froze the smile upon his lips.

Immediately after he had eaten, the boy's education was commenced. The old man was a deaf mute. The boy had no memory of speech. Under these conditions the process of instruction was laborious, but the frightful disposition of the cruel teacher spurred the pupil on to his best efforts that he might escape the terrible beatings that were his almost hourly lot during the strenuous days of his education.

About all that was required of him was to fish for food for themselves and the lion, cook the meals for himself and, the old man, and keep the ship's lights trimmed and burning by night. He soon discovered that his master, the lion, and himself were the only tenants of the drifting derelict.

He never, even to himself, questioned the strange conditions of his life. Except for his brief experiences in the ocean and later in the life boat, he knew no other existence. Insofar as he was aware the deck of the steamer was the universe, and they three the beginning and the end of life.

When he had come aboard, the lion's cage had been a mass of filth; but presently the boy, prompted by a strange liking for cleanliness, had cleaned it out. Thereafter, daily, he reached far in with a broom, and flushed the cage with pails of sea water. The lion was strangely indifferent to his close proximity, though when the old man came near the beast flew into the most frightful rages.

It was not long before the youth discovered the cause of the beast's hatred for the man. The second day of his presence aboard the ship he saw the old fellow creeping stealthily toward the cage with a sharp pointed iron bar in his hands. He crawled upon all fours and upon his hideous features was set an expression of bestial cunning.

The lion saw him at about the same time that the boy did, and with the sight the animal crouched, snarling and moaning, upon the floor of his cage. He lashed his strong tail against the planking, bared his mighty teeth, and as the man came closer backed into the farthermost corner of his prison.

Evidently the thing was but a repetition of previous similar occurrences. It seemed a sort of weird and brutal game that the two were playing—the repulsive and hideous old man mewing and mouthing at the great beast that lashed itself into a frenzy of impotent rage in the far corner of its cage.

Slowly the old man approached. At last he was close to the rusting bars, and then with a maniacal screech he lunged at the lion with his sharp pointed weapon. Screaming and roaring with pain and rage the beast leaped for the tantalizing bar. Between his giant teeth he seized it, but the old man clung tenaciously to his end and each time that the lion loosed his hold to give a fresh roar of anger the tormentor was permitted to prod him once again with the sharp point. The brutal scene endured until the old man became exhausted, and then, mumbling and laughing to himself, he slunk away to hide his weapon in his cabin.

When he had gone the boy approached the cage where the lion lay rumbling out his rage and licking his wounds. The beast was gaunt and mangy from confinement and improper food; but notwithstanding that and its youth it was already a formidable engine of destruction, yet the youth came quite close to it as fearlessly as though it had been a puppy; and extending his hand into the cage stroked its head, purring to it much after the fashion that the lion himself purred when contented.

The boy was sorry for the suffering animal, since he knew by experience the pain that the old man could inflict, as he himself had already twice brought down upon himself the vicious assaults of the ancient defective although he had been but little more than a day upon the derelict.

The lion permitted the child to caress him, and at last his grumbling ceased. His great tongue licked the hand of his little friend and he hugged close to the bars of his cage to be closer to the boy.

Thus the old man found them when he came on deck

later. The sight seemed to arouse his rage once more; and with vicious cuffs and kicks he drove the youth away from the cage, setting him to fishing over the side.

Thus the days ran—long, monotonous days that trailed on into weeks and months, and still the same round of vicious abuse for the lad and the lion. The same hopeless, endless eternity of hate and fear for the hideous old man —the vicious old moron who hovered constantly over them, taking his only pleasure—his fiendish, brutal pleasure—in the sufferings of the two helpless creatures in his power.

But neither the lion nor the boy knew aught else, other than the few moments of quiet they occasionally found in one another's company when the old man chanced to be below. And with the passing days the boy grew in stature and in strength, and the lion grew, too, toward the early maturity that was soon to transform him into a mighty, black-maned beauty.

And the old man, his fits of epilepsy more frequent, grew still more cruel and fiendish. And the day of reckoning approached.

THREE

Once again a man and a boy walked through the gardens of the palace; and when they approached, sentries snapped to attention and presented arms; but outside the great gates no smiling crowds waited to wave and cheer, and there were many more soldiers at the gates than there ever had been before. The man was tense, his steps jerky; his eyes shifted constantly from side to side, apprehensively; his brows were furrowed by an habitual frown. The boy at his side was sullen, his bearing arrogant.

"How much longer do I have to stay cooped up here like a prisoner?" he demanded. "I want to go for a drive. I want to go to the lodge for a week-end."

"You would never reach the lodge, you little fool," snapped the man. "You would be dead before you reached the city limits."

"Are you not king now?" challenged the boy.

"Yes, I am king; but what of it?" demanded the man.

"If I were king, I should go where I pleased, if I had to take the whole army with me. I should have the dogs shot down, if they tried to stop me—what they need is a lesson."

"They had one last Friday," said the man. "That is one of the reasons we had better stay out of the city for a while."

"It was not very much of a lesson," sneered the boy; "the soldiers killed only seven of them. When I am king, I shall kill them all if they don't behave."

"You may be king much sooner than you expect," said the man.

"Why?" demanded the boy.

"Because I listened to poor advice. I hope you will not do the same. Times have changed. Peoples have discovered that they can get what they demand. They demanded a constitutional government with a figurehead king. I didn't give it to them."

Three men sat at a table at a sidewalk cafe. One of them might have been a college professor, one a workingman, and the third, from his military bearing, a soldier. Other diners sat near them, and people were constantly passing close to their table on the sidewalk. They spoke in ordinary conversational tones that anyone listening might have overheard. They did not look nor act like conspirators, yet they were plotting to overthrow a dynasty, to assassinate a king and his son. In the order that I have described them they were Andresy, Bulvik, and Carlyn—A, B, and C—names that will serve our purpose as well as any other, since all names in this story must be fictional. The openness of their plotting bespoke their contempt for the forces of the government, their certainty that the people were with them.

"I think it was Sarnya," said Bulvik. "Otto was the only other one who knew, and he certainly wouldn't have warned the king."

"What proof have you that the king was warned?" asked Andresy.

"He had promised Michael to take him with him that morning when he drove," replied Bulvik. "Michael had asked to drive in the park. We got this direct from one of our agents in the palace; then at the last minute, when the boy was all ready to go, the king refused to take him. Jagst went to the carriage with the old man, and was evidently trying to dissuade him from going. Jagst looked worried. And then what? Why, after it happened Jagst and the boy disappeared. Can't you see that they must have known? Somebody had to tell them. It must have been Sarnya."

"Why should he tell them?" demanded Carlyn. "He was only a captain in the guard under the old king; now he is General Count Sarnya, Chief of Staff."

"Then who could it have been?" demanded Bulvik.

Andresy shook his head. "What is done, is done," he said. "We must profit by our experience. We must not trust any of them. Meyer trusted them and he is dead, and we have a worse king than we had before. Where is our fine new constitution now? We have it all to do over again."

"And it is going to be far more difficult now that Sarnya is Chief of Staff," said Carlyn. "He has the army behind him solidly, for he is as popular with the rank and file as he has always been with the officers. Further-more, he has persuaded Otto to increase the pay right down the line."

"And the people pay," growled Bulvik.

"If Sarnya were eliminated," suggested Andresy, "we might get some place. He has the brains and the courage. Otto has neither."

"I'd kill 'em all," said Bulvik, "Sarnya, Otto, and his nasty little brat, Ferdinand—all of 'em."

Andresy shook his head. "We cannot do that," he said: "we must continue to have a king. If Meyer had lived, it might have been different. He was the only man that all the factions might have been depended upon to rally round. If Sarnya were out of the way, we could control Otto. He's so scared now, since the Good Friday Mas-sacre, that he doesn't dare leave the palace grounds. He'd give us anything we asked if we'd guarantee him safety."

"I will kill Sarnya," said Bulvik. "I swear it!"

"Lessons, lessons, lessons!" grumbled Ferdinand. "I am sick of lessons."

"Well, perhaps you need a rest," said the tutor. "We can go out into the gardens and you can play."

"Play with whom? You?" sneered Ferdinand.

"No, Ferdinand. There is the gardener's son. He is a nice boy."

"I do not play with scum," said Ferdinand.

"Michael used to play with him," replied the tutor.

"I am not Michael."

"I realize that."

"And when you address me, remember that I am Highness."

"Yes, Your Highness."

"Now get out. I'm going into the gardens. I want to be alone."

"But, Your Highness, you should not go alone," objected the tutor. "His Majesty has given strict orders."

"Shut up and get out!" shouted the prince.

"But, Your Maj—" Ferdinand picked up an inkwell and hurled it at the tutor's head.

"Get out and stay out!" he screamed.

"What is it, Carruthers?" asked the king.

"I wish to be relieved," said Carruthers. "I am going back to England."

"Well, what's the trouble? You're the third one in a month. Aren't you being paid enough?"

"He just threw an inkwell at my head, Sir," said the tutor.

"Oh, tut, tut, Carruthers; you must remember he's a very high-strung lad. You must remember, too, that he is crown prince and that some day he will be king—he has certain prerogatives."

"He may exercise them on someone else. Sir. I am leaving."

* * * *

There was a bench in the garden that was partially concealed by shrubbery. However, one could see out into the garden from it although almost concealed oneself. This was a favorite place of Ferdinand's when he went into the garden alone to sulk, as he was doing today. He thought that his lot was a very hard one, and so he felt quite sorry for himself. He wished that he were king, notwithstanding the fact that only through the death of his father could he become king.

Presently his rather handsome, sullen face lighted as something in the garden attracted his attention. It was a girl of about his own age. She was gathering flowers and humming a little tune. She was a very pretty little girl.

"Come here!" commanded Ferdinand.

The girl looked up and around, startled. She could see no one.

"Come here," repeated Ferdinand.

"Where?" asked the girl. "I do not see you."

"Over here under the magnolia tree," directed Ferdinand.

The girl came timidly toward him, and when she saw him she curtsied.

"Come closer," he directed, and when she stood in front of him, "What is your name?"

"Hilda."

"What are you doing in the palace grounds?" demanded the prince.

"My father is employed here."

"He is an official of the palace?" asked Ferdinand. "He is a noble?"

"Oh, no; he is chief gardener."

Ferdinand grimaced. "Nevertheless, you are very pretty," he said. "Do you know who I am?"

"Yes, Your Highness."

"I would not have guessed it from your manner of addressing me," he said, with a trace of sarcasm.

"I do not understand," she said. "Did I do something wrong?"

"People usually say 'Highness' when they reply to my questions," he said.

She started to giggle, but caught herself. "We always called Michael 'Mike'," she said, "but then he was crown prince for so long that he probably got used to it."

Ferdinand flushed. "Well," he said, "when we're alone you may call me Ferdinand."

"Thank you, Highness," she said.

"Sit down," said Ferdinand, moving over on the bench to make room for her. "Do you know you are very pretty?"

"Yes, Highness," she replied.

"I am very lonely," he said. "Talk to me."

"Let me go and get Hans," she suggested. "We can play hide-and-go-seek."

"Who is Hans?" he asked suspiciously.

"My brother."

"Oh," said Ferdinand. "No," he added after a moment's thought. "I may play with you but not with your brother."

"Why?" she asked.

"Because you are a girl. It is all right for a prince or a king to play with a girl of the lower classes but not with boys."

"Why?" she demanded.

"I don't know," he admitted, "but one is always hearing of kings and princes having girl friends whose parents are very low indeed."

For half an hour Ferdinand was almost happy and almost human; then Hilda said that she must go.

"You will come into the garden again tomorrow?" he asked.

"Yes, Ferdinand."

"And every day at this time."

"If I can," she promised.

* * * *

The next day a man came to Martin de Groot, the head gardener, and applied for a position as laborer. He had excellent credentials. They were forged, but Martin de Groot did not know that; so he put him to work, being short-handed because two of his men had been on the streets on Good Friday and been killed by the soldiers. The new man's name was Bulvik.

FOUR

Months rolled into years, and still the drifting derelict pursued her tortuous and erratic course at the behest of current, wind, and tide. That she ever was reported is doubtful, as few ships sighted her that might have guessed that anything was wrong aboard her; and she was no particular menace to navigation as her lights burned brightly by night, and by day only the practiced eye of an attentive mariner could have noted any strangeness about her.

When a ship was sighted whose course might bring it close to the derelict the old man would have the boy light a smudge in the fire box in the boiler room. The passing stranger seeing black smoke issuing from the single funnel, and the ship's nose in the wind, would assume that she had hove to for some minor repairs.

On the few occasions that ships had spoken or desired to board her the deaf mute had run a smallpox flag to the mast head; thus effectually checking the curiosity and enthusiasm of the strangers.

After each such encounter, if the ships had stood close enough to have read the steamer's name upon her stern, the old fellow would laboriously paint it out and rechristen her. At other times he had the boy repaint the hull above the water line—so that the ship was sometimes grey, sometimes black, and again white, while the upper works varied from red to yellow.

Thus, in a way, the derelict usually looked quite spick and span, and, as a consignment of paint had been a part of her cargo at the time of her abandonment, in this respect at least it seemed little likely that she would ever give outward evidence to passing ships that she was a helpless, unmanned vessel.

The boy had never wondered why a ship should be thus aimlessly floating as he had found her with only an old man and a lion aboard her, for remembering nothing of his past existence he assumed without question that this was the only form and manner of life. When he had seen the first ship that approached them after he had become a member of the derelict's strange company, he had been filled with excitement since then it was that he realized that there were other creatures and other ships upon the face of the watery universe that was all he knew; but even then he believed that there could be naught aboard the stranger but old men and lions and boys.

During the years that came and went the old man taught the youth a sort of rude jargon composed of signs and the manual speech of deaf mutes—enough so that he could impart his instructions to his poor little slave. Knowing no spoken language, nor any difference in mentality between himself and the lion, the youth labored diligently to devise a similar system wherewith he and the great cat might converse. In this, of course, he failed; yet there was unquestionably a kind of thought transference, if you will, between the lad and the lion that as the years passed became little short of uncanny, so quickly did each grasp the wishes and intentions of the other.

The vocal attainments of the boy were patterned, naturally, after those of the creature that he loved best. When he was happy and contented, as he usually was when he lay close pressed against the bars of his chum's cage, he purred—a deep, rumbling purr—and when he was angry—when the old man threatened or abused him, he snarled and roared in a way so horrible that had the ancient moron been able to hear he would have been filled with terror for what the savage noise foreboded when the youth should have grown in strength.

Four years had passed. The boy had grown to be a tall, broad-shouldered fellow. The old man, noticing the growth of the great muscles, became more cautious in his abuses. He had fashioned a heavy whip of leather that he had found among the odds and ends of cargo. With this he could inflict the most exquisite torture upon the naked body of the youth, and yet remain beyond the clutch of the strong hands.

Habit performs miracles. The boy knew nothing other than abuse from his master, nor anything but obedience to his will. To have struck back would not have occurred to him—at least not at that time, yet that the thought was growing in his brain was evidenced by the fact that he now resisted abuse—first he had accepted it meekly as the natural order of things from which there was no escape.

One day, a trifle over four years from the time that he had clambered over the steamer's side, a large ship passed close to the derelict. At the old man's signal the boy had built a smudge in the fire box, and then coming upon deck had leaned over the rail to watch the vessel as it steamed by.

To his pleasure and astonishment the ship altered her course to come quite close to the derelict. It was evidently the intention of her master to hail the stranger. The old man, standing upon the bridge, guessed the other's intentions, and leaning over toward the deck gibbered at the boy to attract his attention. When he had succeeded he signalled him to raise the smallpox flag.

At sight of this sinister emblem the stranger again altered his course to pass along upon the derelict's port side and bear away. The maneuver brought the two ships within a hundred yards of one another. Upon the deck of the stranger the youth saw many strange figures—there were men and women and children in strange and wonderful raiment. There were officers and seamen in uniform. But nowhere among them all did he see an old man like his master, or a lion, or a naked youth.

Someone upon the stranger waved a handkerchief toward the derelict, and the youth waved his hand in imitation and roared out a thunderous lion-like greeting. Instantly all eyes were riveted upon the naked figure of the youth.

The officer upon the bridge raised a megaphone to his lips and shouted some query toward the old man upon the derelict's bridge—a query that there was no one upon the drifting vessel to understand.

The old man but pointed to the waving signal at the masthead, and then turning toward the youth shrieked and gibbered at him as he signalled him to go below. The boy was loath to forego the novel sight of all the strange and interesting creatures that had broken upon his astonished vision, and so he ignored the commands of his master.

The ancient one jumped up and down in the frenzy of his rage; and finally rushing to the deck tried to drag the youth below, and now for the first time the spirit of resistance manifested itself. At first the boy but held back as the old fellow attempted to force him from the deck; but when, in the extremity of his anger, the man struck him the boy struck back—a single mighty blow that sent the bearded defective rolling across the deck, where he lay shrieking and frothing at the mouth in a sudden fit of epilepsy.

That the commander of the passing ship knew that all was not right aboard the strange craft was evidenced by his actions. He ordered the engines reversed, and for half an hour he hovered about the vicinity of the derelict as though of half a mind to board her; but at last the menace of the signal at her masthead held him off, and finally he drew away. By the time the old man had recovered from his attack the stranger was hull down upon the horizon.

The old man's first thought upon recovering the use of his limbs was of punishment and revenge. Muttering to himself, he hurried below to return a moment later with his great whip and the iron bar he was wont to use upon the lion those times he worked his fiendish pleasure upon the caged brute.

But now he turned all his attentions toward the youth, who still stood at the rail watching the diminishing silhouette of the vanishing steamer. Like a beast of prey the old man crept stealthily toward his unconscious victim. His close-set eyes glared horribly—the whites showing entirely around the burning pin points of the iris.

Behind him the caged lion watched with narrowed, blazing orbs. The great beast crouched low against the bars of his prison. His lower jaw dropped and raised, dripping saliva upon the planking of the floor between his huge paws. The strong tail lay straight extended behind him, only the sinuous tip flicking nervously back and forth.

The man was almost upon the youth; then the lion rose suddenly to his feet, and from his cavernous jaws broke forth a hideous roar of anger and of warning. Swift as thought the youth wheeled; and at the same instant the old man leaped upon him, striking him with the iron bar and the heavy whip. Down went the boy, while above him, gibbering and shrieking, the awful old man stood raining heavy blows upon his naked, unprotected body.

In high-pitched, hideous laughter the half-crazed epileptic gibbered and mouthed his fiendish glee with each blow that fell upon his defenseless victim. The youth did his best to shield his head from the heavy blows and at the same time to crawl away; but his relentless Nemesis followed close upon him, knocking him back to the deck each time that he essayed to rise.

From behind them rose the hideous roars of the angered lion. The great beast leaped back and forth from one end of its cage to the other. Now it reared upon its hind legs and beat at the bars before it—old, rust-rotted bars that never had been intended to confine a full-grown lion.

But the habit of captivity was so strong upon the beast that it is doubtful that ever before had a desire to pass from its accustomed home impinged upon its brain. Now, however, the lion saw its only friend and companion being slowly beaten to death before its eyes. The savage blood ran furious in its veins. The black mane stood erect upon its back, and down its spine a little ridge bristled with rage; and then of a sudden, with all the great weight of its giant body and all the unthinkable strength of its mighty muscles, the lion hurled himself against the cage's punny bars.

Like straws before a mad bull the frail barrier tumbled away, and with a horrid roar the king of beasts sprang out upon the deck. The old man turned at the sudden nearness of the presence he could not hear. His jaws fell apart in a convulsive grimace of fear. For a moment his knees smote upon one another, and then as the lion crouched for its spring the moron turned and fled toward his cabin.

As well to have leaped for the flaming sun. Scarce a stride had he taken before the beast was upon him. As he fell, he rolled over upon his back. The lion looked down into his wicked face—wide spread jaws gaped horribly above him—the hot and fetid breath of the carnivore beat upon his skin—foam and saliva drooled from the cruel jowls to mingle with the epileptic froth that flecked his beard.

With hideous choking cough the gasping old man was stricken with a spasm of the dire and horrible malady that owned him—and then the mighty jaws of the lion closed full upon his face. When they came away, the face came with them leaving only a bloody smear of brains and broken bones to mark where once the features of a human being had been.

The lad, half stunned by the blows the old man had rained upon him, lay as one dead as the maddened beast mauled and tore what had a few moments before been its cruel master and most hated enemy. Presently he opened his eyes to look full upon the ghastly spectacle.

The lion was devouring the old man—rumbling and snarling over the gruesome, bloody feast. Now the lad, all suddenly, saw his four-footed friend in a new light. Yesterday he had been but a softly purring kitten, rubbing his muzzle lovingly against the boy's hand. Today he was a man-eater—grim, grisly and terrible—and he and the lad were alone upon the deserted ship with no bars between them.

As the boy looked up the lion ceased feeding for a moment and raised his head, his eyes blazing straight into those of the youth. Slowly the young man came to his feet. His first thought was to flee to the safety of the cabin and there barricade himself against this frightful creature—instinct, for so long dormant, had suddenly awakened to give birth to fear.

The lion half closed his eyes, and purring gently moved his great form to half uncover the victim of his rage. His expression and his action constituted an invitation which the boy could not mistake—he had been bidden to the feast!

He shuddered as the full hideousness of the idea possessed him; but at the same time a sudden determination swept over him, and without the slightest evidence of fear or hesitation he walked to the beast's side and grasping the grisly remnants of his master attempted to drag it from the clutches of the beast of prey, at the same time signalling the lion to release the body from his encumbering weight.

For a moment the beast looked in puzzled inquiry at the lad, and then with a low growl he arose and with head cocked questioningly upon one side watched the youth drag the corpse to the ship's side and drop it overboard.

For the next half hour the boy paid not the slightest attention to the animal. After disposing of the body of his torturer he next drew up pail after pail of sea water with which he flushed the deck of the last trace of the tragedy which had so recently been enacted there.

The lion, meanwhile, roamed at will about the ship, enjoying to the full the undreamed possibilities and pleasures of freedom. He had been captured while still a very young cub, and sold to the captain of the steamer which had at that time been lying at anchor in the mouth of a great African river.

On board the ship there had been a stowaway—the ancient defective—and upon him the captain had laid the duty of caring for the lion. From the first the old man had hated the beast as he hated everything else in the universe, and when the captain had discovered and punished one of his cruelties the old fellow's hatred for the cub had developed into an obsession for revenge.

A portion of the mixed cargo of the steamer had consisted of several cases of giant powder, so that when, two weeks after the cub came on board, fire broke out in the hold during a heavy blow the steamer had been abandoned with such haste that the deaf mute, asleep in his hammock, had been entirely forgotten.

He awoke the next morning to find four feet of water sloshing about in the hold of the ship. An open hatch told him how the giant seas had found their way below. He also discovered that besides the cub he was alone upon the steamer. The evidences of fire, which the waves had extinguished, explained why the ship had been abandoned.

His desertion added nothing to the old fellow's love for his fellow man. The ship was well stocked with provisions, and there was an apparatus for distilling fresh water from salt. Under the circumstances, he was not so ill off after all. The result was that he settled down to his new life quite contentedly, preserving the cub for purposes of amusement—torture and revenge.

For six months after the death of the old man the ship continued to drift hither and thither about the broad Atlantic. The boy and the lion lived their lives in peace and happiness. The lad fished for flesh for the lion—porpoises and dolphins affording the warm-blooded flesh of the mammalia that the beast most craved.

After the first moment of horror at the sight of the beast upon the body of the old man the lad had felt no further fear of his huge, black-maned companion. The two ate together, wandered about the ship side by side, and at night slept in the captain's cabin—the huge carnivore close beside the berth in which the lad lay.

One day the boy sighted a strange and wondrous thing beyond the ship's lee rail—it was land! But the lad knew nothing of land. He could but wonder at the strange sight that unfolded before him as the derelict drifted close to the shore. He saw trees and bushes for the first time in the experience of his new memory. He saw a low, sandy beach on which the surf rolled ceaselessly, and in the distance barren hills. He was filled with excitement as he strained his eyes toward this wonderland. Beside him stood the lion, blinking out across the water. Presently he lifted his head to roar forth some pent emotion which the sight of long-forgotten land released.

Slowly the ship drifted before the wind until with a grating of the keel and a slight tremor it came to rest a hundred yards from where the frothy foam washed in undulating lines upon the sand.

It was high tide. With the ebb the steamer commenced to list; and finally she lay upon her side, high and dry, with the sea behind her. Before her two passengers stretched a new world of unguessed romance and adventure.

FIVE

Andresy, Bulvik, and Carlyn did not talk together at sidewalk cafes any more. They were never seen together on the streets at all. When they met it was generally in the back room of a small inn that was run by a friend. Here they could eat and drink and talk unobserved. It was not safe to do that together in public any more since Sarnya had organized his corps of secret military police. They always met evenings now, for Bulvik had a job that kept him occupied during the day. Bulvik and Carlyn were on their second bottle of wine this evening when Andresy came in.

"You are late, brother," said Bulvik.

"Yes," said Andresy. "I thought I was being followed."

"Are you sure you eluded them?" asked Carlyn, fearfully.

"Quite," said Andresy. "I may have been mistaken, but one never knows these days. Sarnya's spics are everywhere."

"Are you sure no one saw you come in here?" demanded Bulvik. "It would be fatal were I to be seen with you, for you are known."

"No one saw me, brother; you may rest assured as to that," Andresy replied confidently. "But how about you? How are you progressing?"

"I am working regularly in the main gardens now," replied Bulvik. "I see the king and Ferdinand almost every day. I could get either of them nearly every day. On some days I could get both of them together. It would be very simple. Oftentimes it is difficult to resist the temptation."

"You have your orders," said Andresy shortly. "We do not want them. It is Sarnya we want. Does he never come into the gardens?"

"Seldom," replied Bulvik. "When he has come, it has been impossible to approach him without arousing suspicion. There are always members of the secret police with him. He is better guarded than the king or the prince. But some day he will pass close to me—too close for his own health."

"You are not suspected?" asked Carlyn.

"No, not at all. They pay no attention to me. As far as Ferdinand and Otto are concerned I might as well be dirt under their feet, the swine. I am told that the old king and Michael used to talk with everyone, but not these two. I should like nothing better than to shoot them both, especially the boy. I think he will be worse than his father. He has more brains and more courage and a worse disposition. He hates the people—calls us scum and dregs and dogs. The only person of our class he even looks at is the gardener's daughter. She is a very pretty girl and growing prettier. If I were her father, I'd slit her throat before I'd let her grow up around the palace."

"But Ferdinand is only a child," objected Andresy.

"Children grow up," said Bulvik, "and oftentimes they are precocious."

"Well, we do not have to worry about that," said Andresy. "We have but one thing to think of now—Sarnya. We can get nowhere while he lives. The next I hear of you, brother, I shall hope to hear that you have fulfilled your mission."

"And that will be the last you will ever hear of me," said Bulvik.

"Your name will live forever, brother," Andresy assured him, "long after Sarnya's is forgotten."

"Much difference it will make to me or to Sarnya," grumbled Bulvik.

* * * * *

"Why is it, Hilda, that the prince will not play with me?" asked Hans. "Mike used to, and we all had such good fun together. Whenever Ferdinand comes around I have to stand up straight and salute, and then he sends me away. Why does he not send you away, too?"

"Because I am a girl," said Hilda.

"What do you and he play?" asked Hans.

"We do not play," said Hilda. "We talk. You see, we are getting grown up. We are older than you or Mike. We talk of many things that you would not understand."

"Fiddlesticks!" said Hans.

"Here he comes now," said Hilda. "You'd better run away and play somewhere else."

"I have no one to play with since Mike went away and Ferdinand keeps you from playing with me. I hate him!"

"You must not say such things! Now run away."

When Ferdinand approached, she curtsied, as he had told her she must in case someone might see them meet; for Ferdinand was a stickler for appearances. Then they went and sat on the bench behind the shrubbery and talked of many things that Hans would not have understood.

Hilda was very pretty and a natural coquette, and Ferdinand was a normal boy approaching adolescence. Also, it was quite secluded on the bench behind the shrubbery. Ferdinand thought no one could see them when he kissed Hilda for the first time, but Hans saw. He had come up from behind them to learn what it was they talked of that he would not understand.

There was another man in the garden not far away,

but he was not particularly interested in them. He was just working and waiting—waiting, hoping, and hating, principally hating. It was Bulvik.

General Count Sarnya had been closeted with the king. Ordinarily he left by the postern door, but today he had ordered one of the palace motors to meet him inside the gates. His own car and police guard waited at the postern gate. Count Sarnya was keeping a rendezvous that he did not wish even his own police to know about—or, perhaps, especially his own police. The system of spying, becomes quite complex eventually because it is necessary to have spies to spy on spies and other spies to spy on the spies who spy on spies. This was what had happened to Count Sarnya's system.

As he walked alone through the palace gardens, Bulvik saw him coming. So did Ferdinand, and he sat very still and drew Hilda farther behind the shrubbery. As Count Sarnya came opposite him, Bulvik suddenly sprang to his feet. There were three revolver shots in quick succession. Hilda screamed; and Hans, unnoticed, fled from his concealment and raced for home.

* * * *

The following evening Andresy and Carlyn sat in the back room of the inn of their friend. They were depressed and glum.

"First Meyer, now Bulvik," said Carlyn, "and nothing accomplished. We are worse off than we were under the old regime. Poor Bulvik! He will not even be classed as a martyr. No one will remember him but you and I."

"To be a martyr," said Andresy, "one should first be a good shot. He missed Sarnya completely, I understand; and Sarnya shot him twice in the heart before he could fire again."

SIX

The lad and the lion entered northern Africa at a point where the desert comes closest to the sea. As they wandered away from the ocean, walking side by side, the youth at the lion's shoulder, they were bent merely upon an expedition of discovery—at least this was true of the boy.

About him were strange and wonderful sights that filled him with amazement and delight. The broad stretches of open, rolling country; the hills in the distance; the trees and bushes—all seemed a veritable fairyland to one who had never before dreamed that anything but a dreary waste of tumbling water lay beyond the narrow confines of the drifting derelict that had been his world.

Far to the right the lad saw the dark green of dense foliage winding toward the hills. It was the jungle which clothed the banks of a little river that wound down to the sea. Beyond the mountains lay the desert, but of that the lad knew nothing. Just now he was engrossed with those things which were already before his wondering eyes.

He bent his steps toward the distant jungle, and beside him paced the great lion, now full-grown and in his prime —a mighty beast of prey, yet still unmindful either of his great strength or of the purpose for which it was intended. The youth, too, had matured. The last few months had witnessed a development in the lad little less marked than that which had taken place in the lion. Each was a splendid specimen of his kind—the two naked beasts who

43

walked side by side and unafraid into the savage wilderness of an unknown world.

They were moving up wind, and presently there was wafted down to the sensitive nostrils of the lion a strange and delightful aroma. Up went his massive head. Straight behind extended his long, supple tail, the bushy tuft twitching nervously at the extremity. He gave a low whine, and at the same instant the boy's eyes fell upon that which the lion's scent had first perceived—a little herd of antelope grazing in a hollow just beyond them.

Here was meat. The impatient lion stalked rapidly through the low bushes that extended to within a hundred yards of the quarry. The boy, more in imitation of his companion than because he realized as yet the necessity for stealth, bent low beside his tawny chum, creeping forward with him, and to better hold his crouching position one smooth brown arm lay about the mighty shoulders of the beast of prey.

The two came to the edge of the bush without attracting the attention of the antelope. From here on there was no shelter. With a deafening roar the lion leaped into the clearing, racing toward his prey; but the frightened creatures wheeled and were away before the mighty claws could fasten themselves upon a single one.

The lion's sudden charge had left the youth behind—his human muscles could not hope to cope with the speed of his companion—but for a few moments the two raced futilely after the fast-disappearing herd.

Twice again that day did they come thus tantalizingly close to luscious repasts only to be robbed of them at the last moment by the superior speed of their intended victims. Then it was that the superior intelligence of the boy commenced to assert itself. He saw that only by accident could they ever capture one of the fleet and wary

44

creatures unless they could come unseen sufficiently close for the lion to spring upon it with a single bound. Without cover there seemed little likelihood that this would happen.

He had noticed how quickly the antelope turned and fled in the opposite direction from that form which he and the lion approached them. This gave him an idea, and as they sighted another small herd just before they came to the jungle he put his plan to test.

The lion, as before, was creeping stealthily toward the grazing creatures, taking advantage of some bushes that intervened. When he reached the end of the shelter he would have sprung out, roaring, only to frighten away the quarry; but this time the boy clutched the heavy mane, and through the strange speech medium that had been slowly developing between these two during the years of their companionship, he made the lion understand that he was to remain where he was, hidden behind a little clump of bushes some two hundred yards from the herd.

Then the boy, taking advantage of such cover as he could find, circled the antelope until he had come to a point beyond them and directly opposite the lion. Here he was up wind from them with the result that they quickly got his scent. He was surprised to note their sudden alarm before they could by any possibility have seen him. He had not yet learned the wondrous possibilities of the sensitive organs of smell with which the creatures of the wild are endowed. His intention had been to show himself to the antelope—how they knew of his presence before they could see him was a mystery to him, though it was not many days before he guessed the truth and took advantage of it upon every occasion.

Now as the startled herd stood looking in his direction with upcocked ears, he sprang up in full view of them, shouting and waving his arms. Terrified, the animals stampeded straight away from him—directly toward the crouching lion. Behind them raced the lad. He saw a fine buck leaping straight for the very bush that concealed his fierce hunting mate. He heard a sudden, frightful roar, and saw the tawny, black-maned king of beasts spring full upon the breast of the buck.

Great teeth buried themselves in the soft throat, down went the quarry; and the remainder of the herd scattered to right and left to pass out of sight in the distance before ever they diminished their speed. The boy ran up to where the lion was already busy with his feast, growling as he tore the tender flesh and drank the hot, delicious blood.

As the youth approached the lion looked up, his great jaws dripping red with gore. He bared his mighty fangs in instinctive resentment of interference with his feast, but as the lad pounced upon the buck's haunch, burying his teeth in the flesh and tearing out a great mouthful, the lion made no move to dispossess him. Instead, he but turned again to the filling of his own belly, and so the two feasted upon their kill until both were satisfied.

Thus the two learned, little by little, to hunt together —the brain of the man and the brawn of the beast working together to insure their supremacy in the hills, the jungle and the fringe of forest beyond the hills to which they sometimes extended their activities.

They laired within a dark cave in the hillside near the source of the river they had perceived that first day winding its graceful way down to the sea. The mouth of their den was hidden by a thicket of scrubby bushes, and the way to it led upward along a narrow path and a tiny ledge—it was a most impregnable fortress and had been chosen from several others by the superior mind of the youth.

Thus they lived only to fill their bellies and to sleep; knowing or caring, yet, for no other manner of existence. At times the boy was restless, wandering through hill and jungle by day as the lion slept. They usually hunted toward dusk, and sometimes after dark; but then the man was handicapped by the limitations of his human sight, though for the eyes of the lion there is no night.

As the youth wandered one afternoon in the ravine below the lair where the lion lay sleeping, his now acute perceptive faculties became suddenly aware of the presence of another creature. Instantly he was on the alert, and a moment later he saw the wicked eyes of a lion peering at him from the depth of a thicket.

Between himself and the safety of his den lay the little river and the strange lion. About him was no place of shelter that he could reach in time, should the lion charge. He and his companion had killed enough to teach the boy that all within the boundary of their little world were enemies, so he had no doubt but that the stranger was stalking him for food.

Slowly now the enemy was creeping toward him, belly to the earth. He was a terrible, an awe-inspiring creature. The youth had never before realized what a frightful thing a full-grown lion really was, for never before had he had experience of another than his own loved companion.

If he were but there now—this fellow would never dare to threaten the lion's chum. With the thought came the sudden hope that he might yet summon his friend. Raising his head he gave vent to a high pitched scream, more cat-like than human. The lion paused in startled amazement. Behind him, up the side of the opposite cliff there appeared to the boy's watching eyes the massive face of his fierce friend, framed in the shaggy blackness of his great mane.

Quickly the eyes of the lion took in the scene below him. The stranger was again approaching the boy when from behind and above him rang out a hideous roar, and as he turned in the direction of this new sound he saw a mighty beast bounding in great leaps down the rocky hillside toward him.

The hunting lion thought that this huge fellow was coming to rob him of his prey, and for a moment he was undecided as to whether he had better secure his meal first and then look to the intruder, or at once turn and do battle with the latter. But whatever his decision it was not given to him to exercise his own volition in the matter, for while he still hesitated the tawny, roaring thing in his rear was upon him.

Then it became evident to him that this creature was bent upon destroying him rather than the luscious meal which still stood within easy reach of either of them. The strange lion was young and strong; but he was no match for the mighty beast that flew at him with wide distended jaws and bared talons.

The fight that followed sent the naked youth dancing with frantic excitement about the contestants. Beside him he discovered a broken branch lying upon the ground. This he seized and with it in his hand danced in and out about the rolling, rending beasts, delivering blows upon any portion of the enemy that gave itself to his view for a sufficient length of time.

He inflicted but little damage upon the object of his attack, for the branch was rotten, and a piece broke off each time it fell upon the foe; but in another way his aid was beneficial, for the effect it had upon the enemy to see his quarry turn upon him and fight side by side with another lion so mystified him that at the first opportunity he disengaged himself from the battle and leaped away as fast as he could go.

The youth, however, thought that he and his stick had defeated the brute; and the idea thus imparted worked within his active brain until he felt the necessity of possessing a long, stout cudgel with which to defend himself against his enemies.

His companion had been rather severely mauled during the fracas, though not nearly so badly as the lion that had fled; but the wounds soon healed and within a short time the two were hunting together as before.

Not long after this, the youth chanced to come upon the same lion that had recently stalked him; but this time the creature fled at sight of him; and little by little, as the two savage hunters came in contact with the other fiercer denizens of their world, their reputations grew until at sight of them, or when their hunting cries broke the stillness of the jungle or the desert, beasts slunk away to hide themselves from the unconquerable two.

Sometimes their quarry led them out into the desert beyond their wild hills; and once they wandered far across the burning sands, the youth leading the way, his growing imagination filled with a haunting desire to fathom what lay behind the broad and endless barrenness of the vast waste.

Topping a sandy hill, the youth descried a lone antelope moving nervously across their path, looking back from time to time as though in expectation of pursuit. As the general direction of the creature's advance would bring it close to where the two stood, the youth dragged the lion down behind the crest of the sandy hill, himself lying flat beside his companion.

Only the tops of their heads and their savage eyes appeared above the sand, and so motionless were these that they might not be seen by the animal moving quickly in their direction.

The antelope was still a couple of hundred yards from them when the figure of a white robed horseman suddenly topped the summit of another hill behind it. Instantly the antelope broke into a run, but simultaneously the man raised a long black stick to his shoulder—there was a puff of smoke from its tip, followed by a great roaring sound, and as though struck by lightning the fleet animal tumbled headlong to the sand.

Immediately a half dozen other horsemen galloped into view beside him who had made the kill. The boy was filled with wonderment and awe. Never had he seen such strange creatures—he thought the men and their ponies inseparable from one another—parts of one individual. His surprise brought him to his feet in full view of the galloping Arabs. For a moment they paused in wonder at the vision of the naked youth silhouetted against the burning desert sky; then, abandoning their kill for the moment, they spurred their fleet mounts in the lad's direction.

But at a hundred yards from him they came to a sudden halt, for then from behind the sandy hill upon which the boy stood and directly at his side rose the massive head of a great black-maned lion. For a moment the Arabs paused in breathless excitement, expecting momentarily to see the youth torn to pieces by the mighty beast beside him.

Then the lion, rumbling forth a deep-throated roar,

paced majestically toward them; and to their horror and astonishment they saw the youth walk forward by the beast's side, one hand grasping the shaggy mane.

The lion had his eyes upon the dead quarry of which he thought the men purposed robbing him. One of the Arabs raised his rifle to fire upon the lion. The youth, having seen the effects of this strange weapon upon the antelope, guessed the man's intention; and springing ahead of his companion, leaped, roaring and growling, toward the astonished Arab.

The sight of the savage, naked beast-man charging down upon him was too much for the son of the desert. With a cry of alarm he wheeled the pony, and followed by his companions galloped rapidly away in the direction from which they had appeared.

Then the lad and the lion settled down to feast upon the carcass of the antelope; but all the while the former's mind was active with the imaginings the sight of the Arabs had aroused within it. As the men had approached closer to him he had seen that they were not a part of their horses—that they sat astride these beasts, and were themselves the same manner of creature as himself and the old man of the derelict and those whom he had seen upon the deck of the steamer that had once approached so close to the drifting vessel that had been his world for so many years.

Another thing that he thought upon as he feasted upon the kill was the fact that he alone of all the other creatures of his kind that he ever had seen went naked. He recalled that upon the day he had come into the world he had been covered with similar strange, removable hide, and that because it had been wet and uncomfortable he had removed it. Evidently it was intended that those who went upon two legs instead of four should be thus adorned—it was a matter that he should have to look into.

Just now he was anxious to be off upon the trail of the men. He wanted to follow them to their lair and see how they lived—to discover where they obtained the beautiful, gleaming coverings they wore. He was all excitement. It seemed to him that the lion would never be done filling his belly.

But at last he succeeded, much to the lion's disgust, in dragging his unwilling companion upon the trail of the Arabs. It led across the barren waste of sand straight away from their cool jungle home. The lion followed it by scent, the boy by the prints of the ponies' feet—not yet effaced by the shifting sand, for there was little breeze blowing at the time.

At dusk they came in sight of a distant clump of date palms among which were nestled some forty goat-skin tents. The wind blew gently from the direction of the camp, wafting to the nostrils of the carnivore the delicious aroma of horses, camels, men, and goats. He raised his giant muzzle and sniffed in the delicate fragrance.

The lion was for going directly down to the quarry, for he had been torn away from the antelope before he had entirely satisfied his hunger. The result was that he was ill natured and savage; but the youth grasped him by the mane, and though he bared his great fangs and growled ominously, in the end he lay down as the lad directed.

The latter wished to feast his eyes upon the sight below him—the habitation of many men, the first of the kind that he had ever seen. Until darkness blotted out the scene he watched the distant figures of men and women coming and going between the tents. He saw the little parties of horsemen which galloped out of the desert haze to dismount and unsaddle before their tents. He saw the camels driven in and penned within the douar. The sight filled him with a strange and unaccountable longing—vague yearnings, for what he knew not—the first seeds of dissatisfaction and discontent with his present lot.

At last the lion could be restrained no longer. Rising, he paced restlessly back and forth, sniffing the scent laden air as he kept his blazing eyes upon the camp.

At last he halted, and raising his great head, gave mouth at first to a low, uncanny moan which presently rose to the fierce and savage thunder of the roar of the hunting lion.

SEVEN

It was the seventeenth birthday of Prince Ferdinand. He and the king were no longer prisoners in the palace. They went abroad almost as they pleased, though they were always well guarded. The iron hand of General Count Sarnya had kept peace in the kingdom, an armed, suspicious peace that had filled the jails and the cemeteries with "Martyrs" and "friends of the people" and other witless ones who got no thanks for their pains and seldom even a decent burial.

Ferdinand enjoyed the pomp and ceremony attendant upon the celebration of this anniversary. He loved the fawning and the eulogizing. He would probably have loved it even had he known that it was false, but he did not. He was too self-centered and egotistical to realize how cordially he was hated. He would not have cared much, had he known; for he looked with contempt upon all creatures below him in rank; and some day he would be king—highest of all. He loved only one person besides himself—Hilda; but he hated many. He hated Sarnya, because Sarnya was more powerful than he. He hated him and feared him. When he became king, he promised himself, Sarnya would be replaced. He even planned on disgracing him.

He hated his father, too, partly because his father feared Sarnya even more than he did, and partly because his father, by living, prevented Ferdinand from becoming king. He had a few friends among the sons of the nobility; but perhaps it would be better to say acquaintances, for these all hated him cordially. Among these, the closest to him was young Count Lomsk, an archsycophant of his own age who was already dissolute and lecherous.

As the long day gave way to evening and the evening drew toward a close, even Ferdinand became bored. He and Max Lomsk put their heads together and sought for a plan of escape. The king had already withdrawn, which made it possible for Ferdinand to do likewise. Lomsk went into the gardens after Ferdinand had retired to his apartments, and presently Ferdinand joined him there. It was not late, and there were still lights in the gardener's cottage at the far end of the palace grounds. The two youths stopped in the shadows of some shrubbery that grew near the cottage; then Ferdinand whistled.

Hans de Groot, who had been admitted to the Royal Military Academy, was home on leave. He heard the whistle and recognized it. He remembered the first time he had seen Ferdinand kiss Hilda. It had been only something to laugh about then; now it was quite different— Hilda was sixteen and Ferdinand seventeen. Now he heard Hilda's door open and close. He listened. Yes, the back door of the cottage was cautiously opened and as cautiously closed again. Hans could stand it no longer—Crown Prince or not, he was going to have it out with Ferdinand. He had no right to compromise Hilda in this way. Hans jumped out of bed and into his uniform as quickly as he could, but when he reached the garden he could see nothing of Hilda or Ferdinand—not even at the bench where they had met in years past. He hurried through the garden toward the palace and as he passed the great gates he saw a girl and two men enter a limousine and drive away. The girl was Hilda, and one of the men was Ferdinand.

There was a sudden tightening of the muscles of Hans' heart. A wave of nausea surged through him as he realized his helplessness. He could not follow them, for he had neither automobile nor money. He paced up and down the garden, determined to wait until they returned; and there was murder in his heart.

The car stopped in the city and picked up the pretty daughter of a cobbler; then it drove on out into the country to the hunting lodge in the woods. There were always servants and food and wine at the hunting lodge.

* * * *

"I tell you," said Carlyn, "that we have got to do something. Our people are becoming discouraged. We must do something to give them new hope."

"What would you suggest?"

"If we could get a promise out of Ferdinand that he would kick Sarnya out and grant us the new constitution when he became king, that would be something," said Carlyn.

"And what would we offer Ferdinand in return?"

"The crown and his life. He would be glad to rule without constant fear of assassination."

"He would probably want to know just how we were going to hand the crown over to him," suggested Andresy. "Had you thought of that?"

"It would be only in the event that an accident befell his father. I have it on good authority that the two dislike one another most cordially and that Ferdinand is anxious to become king; so it might not be too difficult to obtain his co-operation."

"I wonder if he would keep his promises to us," mused Andresy.

"His life would be the stake."

"I am commencing to wish," said Andresy, "that we had left well enough alone. The old king was a good king and Michael was a fine lad. If we only had him here now."

"Well, we haven't. There is no question but that he is dead. Old Jagst's body was found floating in his life belt; so we are sure that Michael went down with the ship, even though his body was never found. There were two hundred others that were never found, and no one has ever suggested that any of them might be alive."

"Meyer was too rabid and too radical," said Carlyn. "He wanted to accomplish everything at a single stroke. I can see now that he was wrong."

"Meyer wanted to be dictator," said Andresy. "He was mad for power, and too anxious to obtain it quickly. That came first with Meyer, the welfare of the people second. It is strange what small, remote things may affect the destiny of a nation."

"What do you mean?" asked Carlyn.

"Because Meyer, as a child, was suppressed and beaten by his father; because, on that account, he had a feeling of inferiority, he craved autocratic power that would permit him to strike back in revenge. Meyer did not realize it himself; but whenever he struck at government, he was striking at his father. When he ordered the assassination of the king, he was condemning his father to death in revenge for the humiliation and brutalities the father had inflicted on him. Now the king is dead and Michael and Meyer and Bulvik and hundreds of the men and women who believed in Meyer; but Meyer's father is still alive, basking in the reflected glory of his martyred son. Life is a strange thing, Carlyn. Civilization is strange and complex. The older I grow the more I realize how little any of us know what it is all about. Why do we strive? Everything we attain always turns out to be something we do not want, and then we try to change it for something else that will be equally bad. Oh, well, but I suppose that we must keep on. How do you plan to kill the king?"

Carlyn started, as though caught red-handed in a crime. "God!" he exclaimed. "Don't spring it on me like that."

Andresy laughed. "You have nerves, haven't you? I never would have believed it. I shall put it in a more emasculated style. What accident will befall the king? and how will it happen?"

"It will take a little time, thanks to Sarnya's most efficient guarding of his royal meal ticket," replied Carlyn; "but I have a plan. First we must approach Ferdinand and obtain his promise of the reforms we desire; then I must be reinstated in the army. That can, I think, be accomplished through the influence of Ferdinand. It was only the little matter of a gambling debt anyway that got me cashiered. I shall try to get back into the Guard; then, some day I shall be detailed for duty inside the palace grounds. That is all I ask."

"That, and a decent burial?" asked Andresy.

"I shall not be caught. I am not so anxious as was Bulvik to become a martyr."

* * * *

It was after midnight, the birthday guests had departed, but the king was still closeted with Sarnya when the officer of the guard asked for an audience.

The king looked up at him irritably. "What now?" he demanded. "Can't you perform your duties without annoying me?"

"I am sorry, Your Majesty," said the officer; "but I thought I should report this to you personally."

"Well, what is it?" snapped the king.

"Prince Ferdinand's valet has informed me that His Royal Highness is not in his apartments and that he cannot locate him anywhere in the palace."

"Has he looked in the garden?" demanded the king.

"I think not, Sir."

"Search the grounds, then; and report back to me."

Hans de Groot paced back and forth in the shadows of the trees and shrubbery that his father had tended and nursed for many years. The white heat of his first anger had passed. He felt cold now, cold with bitterness and resentment and hate. He had always hated Ferdinand, ever since he could remember; but never before had he wanted to kill him.

He saw someone approaching from the palace, and drew back farther into the shadows. As the figure passed nearer one of the new night lights in the gardens, Hans saw that it was that of an officer, and that he was evidently searching the grounds. He was coming in Hans' direction; and the youth, not wishing to be discovered, drew back farther among the bushes. It was this movement that revealed him to the searcher.

"Hey, there!" called the officer. "Who's that?" Hans did

not answer. "If it is you, Your Highness, say so: and come out. If you don't, I shall have to shoot."

"You don't have to shoot," said Hans. "I'll come out." He walked toward the officer.

"Who are you?" demanded the latter.

"I am Hans de Groot. My father is chief gardener."

"What are you doing here?"

"I could not sleep. I was just walking," replied Hans.

"You were not walking; you were hiding. Why did you hide?" Hans made no reply. "You had better answer me or you will get into trouble. Have you seen Prince Ferdinand in the gardens?" Still Hans kept silent. The Dutch are a determined race, not easily coerced. "Very well then, come with me. There are ways to make you speak. You are under arrest."

It is one thing to defy a captain of the guard; quite another to defy a king. Hans was trembling with nervousness when he found himself facing Otto.

"What were you doing in the gardens this time of night?" demanded the king.

"I—I was waiting for my sister to come home."

"Where is your sister?"

"I don't know, Sir."

The king's eyes narrowed. "Who is she with?"

"I—I please, Your Majesty, I would rather not say," stammered the unhappy Hans. It was one thing to demand an accounting himself; quite another to be forced to inform on Ferdinand and Hilda. He had much pride, too. He did not want the king to know that Hilda had— oh, what had she done? Maybe she had done nothing wrong. Hans wished that his father had never left Holland; that he, Hans was dead; that he had never been born.

"It doesn't make any difference what you would rather do," thundered the king. "Who is she with?"

"She was with two men," faltered Hans.

"Who are they?"

"It was quite dark, Your Majesty; and I was not close. They jumped into a limousine and drove away before I could reach the gates."

"Was one of them Prince Ferdinand?" Otto almost shouted.

Hans nodded. "Y—yes, Your Majesty."

* * * *

"I think we should go home," said Hilda. "It is very late. If my father catches me getting in at this hour, I don't know what he might do."

"It is only one o'clock," objected Max, "just the beginning of the evening. We haven't had any fun at all yet. What do you suppose we brought you girls out here for, anyway?—to turn right around and go back?"

"Aw, come on, Hilda, don't be a spoil-sport," urged Ferdinand, drawing the girl down on the sofa beside him and kissing her.

It was then that the door opened and the king and Sarnya stepped into the room.

* * * *

"I wonder," said one undergardener to another, "why they discharged de Groot. He was a fine fellow and a splendid gardener. They will look a long time before they find his equal."

"There is no accounting for what kings do," said his fellow.

EIGHT

When Ben Saada rode back with his fellows to the douar of the Sheik Ali-Es-Hadji and narrated the wondrous story of the naked white youth who hunted in company with *el adrea* of the black mane, the men and the girls laughed at him, saying that fear of *the lord with the large head* had distorted his vision.

And chief amongst the scoffers was Nakhla, the beautiful bronze daughter of Sheik Ali-Es-Hadji. Now, to Ben Saada nothing could have exceeded the humiliation of arousing the laughing scorn of this loveliest daughter of the desert, for he had been paying assiduous court to the maiden for many months; and so, scowling his displeasure, he sulked away to his tent, cursing the moment that his eyes had fallen upon the naked figure of the stranger.

When dark had fallen, and the roar of el adrea rumbled across the desert, Ben Saada came forth from his tent; and, pointing out into the night, dared the men among the laughers to go forth and see for themselves whether or not his story were true; but none ventured to take up his challenge. Instead they fired their long muskets and beat upon tom-toms to frighten the lion away from their flocks and herds.

Out across the sand, the lad and the lion crept slowly down upon the douar. The sound of the guns gave them pause for a time, but at last they resumed their stealthy approach, for by this time the youth was himself hungry, and the scent of the ruminants fell gratefully upon his savage nostrils. Then, too, he wished a nearer view of these creatures of his own kind, for he was imbued with the insatiable curiosity that belongs to all highly intelligent creatures.

Close to the tents the hunters crept, silent now, for they had learned of late that a noisy stalk frightens away the prey. Behind the rude barricade which corraled the Arab's flocks, the two crouched waiting for the din of drum and musket to cease, for they felt a distinct menace to themselves in these hideous noises.

Finally the Arabs quieted down, cajoled into the belief that they had frightened el adrea away. It was quite dark now, and except for a few lolling about a fire the tribesmen had retired to their tents for the night. The time had come. The lad standing upon the shoulders of the lion could just see above the barrier. All was quiet. With a low word to his companion he vaulted over into the corral. Close behind him leaped the lion.

Instantly there was a mad stampede among the animals of the douar. They dashed frantically about the enclosure. Presently the bleat of a sheep and the shrill scream of a stricken horse marked where the two marauders were making their kills.

The men at the fire leaped to their feet, staring wide-eyed toward the corral. After all, el adrea had come. Raising their guns they fired into the air. One piled more wood and camel dung upon the fire—it is not pleasant to be left in the dark when el adrea is near—el adrea who knows no night.

The shots but brought answering growls from the corral. Other white robed figures came silently from their tents, long, grim muskets full cocked for any emergency. The animals within the corral were quieter. There was less mad racing about the enclosure. Occasionally a horse snorted or a camel grunted. Toward the center of the enclosure two beasts of prey stood astride their kills. The lad was the first to move. Just as the rising moon, topping the barrier's summit, flooded the corral with light he swung the carcass of a sheep to his broad shoulder and trotted toward the wall.

The Arabs were standing now before their tents waiting for a sight of the intruders and a shot at them. They were sure that there were two lions—they heard two growling; but Ben Saada insisted that presently they should see—that one was a man.

Even as he spoke, the figure of a naked giant leaped to the top of the corral wall. The brilliant moonlight shone full upon him—there could be no mistake. Even Nakhla had to admit that she had been wrong in laughing at Ben Saada. Upon the giant's shoulder lay the carcass of a sheep—one of Sheik Ali-Es-Hadji's sheep—yet so spellbound were the Arabs by what they saw that none thought to fire.

Scarcely had the man leaped to the open beyond the wall than a great black-maned lion sprang out of the corral directly behind him, and across the lion's mighty shoulders rested the carcass of a black stallion. Even then the Arabs did not shoot—too full were their minds with surprise and awe—and the lad and the lion trotted off across the weird, moon-bathed desert to devour their prey at a safe distance from the douar.

Often thereafter came the two to the douar of Sheik Ali-Es-Hadji. Not because they could not find prey in plenty closer to their own savage lair; but because the youth found a strange, incomprehensible pleasure in being near to creatures of his own kind. He did not, of course, understand property rights, or that he had no business stealing the goats of Sheik Ali-Es-Hadji.

He was perfectly primitive. To him, might was right. He knew that the odd and fascinating white-robed horsemen would kill him could they do so. They were his enemies, as was every other living thing except the great chum of his childhood. He had learned all that he knew of men from the ancient defective. Thus, naturally, he had come to hate and fear creatures like himself. Because of this, it was incomprehensible to him that he longed to be close to them. When he was awake his thoughts were never for long upon any other subject.

And among the people of the isolated douar he, in turn, was the subject of continual wonder and speculation. Ben Saada now had the laugh upon his fellows, and he made the most of it. Nakhla, though she had been the loudest and most merciless scoffer, alone escaped his chaff, for Ben Saada looked with covetous eyes upon the beauteous daughter of his sheik and so could not chance offending her by his raillery.

So profound an impression had the sight of the naked man hunting with a huge lion made upon the Arabs that even the men feared to go abroad other than in parties of several even by day. The women were kept close to the douar, and about the flocks and herds was thrown a guard sufficient even to war time.

Nakhla alone seemed untouched by the fear that possessed her father's people. Lions had never kept her cooped up within the douar, she reasoned, so why should a single, unarmed man in company with a lion cause them such perturbation? For her part, she should go and come as she had always done. The idea! She, the daughter of the great Sheik Ali-Es-Hadji, afraid to venture out upon the desert of her birth. It was preposterous.

And so it happened that one day the spoiled daughter of the sheik rode out alone into the desert carrying word of the coming of a great caravan to her father who rode westward looking to the grazing grounds of his flocks.

It was noon when she reached a rugged little valley in the mountains not a great distance from the sea, but she had not found her sire. The sheik, after leaving the douar, had changed his plans, riding to the south instead of to the west.

Hot and thirsty from the long ride the girl welcomed the sight of the little stream winding along its rocky bed in the center of the valley. Slipping from her saddle she bent low above the water to drink, while her mount, his forefeet in the pebbly brook just below her, buried his muzzle in the clear, cold water.

Neither saw the wondering eyes of the man, or the gleaming, yellow orbs of the great lion watching them from the concealment of a dense thicket upon the flank of an opposite hill. It was the horse which first detected the nearness of danger. An eddying breeze brought down the scent of his keen nostrils, and with a sudden snort he reared backward, jerking the bridle rein from Nakhla's hand. The girl sprang to her feet, leaping toward the animal's head; but with terror-wide eyes the slim Arab wheeled away, his hoofs clattering upon the rocks of the drinking place, and an instant later, with high held head, was galloping back in the direction from which they had come.

Nakhla was far from terror-stricken. She was the brave daughter of a brave sire. All her short life had been spent among the dangers of the desert and the hills. But yet she knew that her position now was most precarious. There could be but one explanation of the sudden, mad fright of El Djebel; and she looked quickly about in search of the lion she knew must be near by.

Her quick, intelligent eyes scanned the surroundings with speed, yet minutely. Presently they were riveted upon a dense thicket far up the opposite side of the ravine.

She had seen a slight movement there; and now, even as she looked, the mighty head of a great, black-maned lion emerged from the tangle.

There were trees near at hand which Nakhla could climb out of harm's way; but there was the possibility that El Djebel would stop to graze after his first terror had been spent, and that by following she might overtake and catch him. That would be far better. There was also good reason to believe that the lion would not follow her, as comparatively few lions are man-eaters. It was worth putting to the test, and anyway there were numerous trees along her path to the head of the canyon and up the hillside to the point over which she must cross to regain the desert.

Quickly, yet without apparent haste, the girl walked in the direction taken by her fleeing mount. Occasionally she cast a backward glance toward the lion. Soon she saw him emerge from the thicket—slowly, majestically. She looked about to locate the nearby trees best suited to her purposes of safety. There were plenty which she could reach in time should el adrea take up the pursuit in earnest.

Again she glanced over her shoulder to discover if the beast had increased his speed. This time her heart sank, for she not only saw that the lion was really stalking her but that at the beasts's side walked the terrible human beast that had robbed her father's flocks and filled the hearts of her people with terror.

Hope was gone. The trees might keep her from el adrea, but not from the reach of his companion. She broke into a faster walk now, hoping to overtake her horse before he again got sight or wind of the lion. She dared not run for fear that it would precipitate an immediate charge upon the part of the two that stalked her.

Every few steps she turned a backward glance toward the grim and silent figures creeping in her wake. They seemed only to be keeping pace with her. As yet, there was no appreciable diminution of the distance between them and her. Yet they were close enough for all that—far too close for comfort.

She could see the man quite plainly—that he was a young white man, superbly muscled, with head and features strong and finely moulded, and with the carriage of a proud and haughty sheik. The sight of him, even then, did not fail to move her both to admiration and to wonder. Yet she feared him, if the daughter of Sheik Ali-Es-Hadji could know fear.

A turn in the canyon presently shut the two from her view; and instantly the girl broke into a run, glancing back the while that she might at once fall into a walk again when the two came once more in sight of her, for she did not wish to invite a charge.

The youth who stalked her had been filled with curiosity at first when he had seen her. But that strange, uncanny telepathy wherewith he was wont to communicate with his savage mate he had held the lion from charging —he wished to examine this creature more minutely.

Nor had his eyes rested upon her face and figure for any considerable time before he found curiosity giving place to wonder at the beauty of the girl. His heart beat so rapidly as his eyes feasted upon her charms that he could feel its pounding against his ribs, and through his whole being surged a rhapsody of emotion that was as unique in his experience as it was pleasurable.

He had never given much thought to the ethics of man-killing, since only once had his companion killed a man, and as that had been in preservation of the youth's life he had naturally felt only gratitude to the huge beast for its act. Something had caused him to interfere when he had found the lion devouring his human kill. He had had no idea why the thing should have seemed so repulsive to him; but it had, and even now he was determined that the lion should not devour the girl. Of course, all things were their enemies; so it was only right that they should be killed; but before killing this one he wished to observe her further.

A second turn in the canyon kept the girl still from the sight of the trailers even after they had rounded the first obstruction; and it also brought her under the eyes of a half dozen vicious looking sons of the desert—ragged, unkempt looking villains, far different in appearance from the splendid warriors of her father's tribe.

She did not see them at first—they were just filing down a narrow trail from the ridge at her right—but they saw her, and the sight brought them to a sudden halt. Furtively they looked about in every direction as though seeking her companions; and then, far up toward the head of the canyon, they saw that which explained the presence of the girl there on foot as well as her probably defenseless condition—a riderless horse scrambling up the steep and rugged path that leads out of the canyon and across the hills to the great desert.

At sight of it the men charged down upon the girl, the rattling of the stones beneath their horses' hoofs attracting her attention. At first she was overjoyed at this timely appearance of armed men; but a second glance brought a pallor to her face, for she saw that these were enemies to be feared a thousand times more than the two behind her. They were the lawless, vicious marauders of the desert—outlawed murderers and criminals, at whose hands there awaited her a fate worse than death—a horrid fate that would end in the harem of some brutal black sultan of the far south.

She turned and ran toward the opposite side of the canyon, hoping to scale the precipitous side, where the mounts of her pursuers could not follow, and hide among the hills until chance should permit her to make her way across the desert to her father's douar or until the help came that she knew would be upon the way the moment El Djebel should gallop, riderless, among the tents of her people.

She almost forgot the man and the lion in the real terror she felt for the cruel and savage human beasts who pursued her; but when she did recall them it was with the hope that the sight of so many horsemen would frighten them away from further stalking her.

As she reached the canyon wall she found to her chagrin that it was too steep at that point to scale, and as she ran along its base searching for a foothold the marauders were upon her. Swinging from his mount the leader caught her in his arms, only to have the girl turn upon him with tooth and nail defending her virtue with the savage ferocity of a lioness protecting its young.

It was upon this sight that the eyes of the youth fell as he rounded the final rocky shoulder that had hid the girl from his view. Instantly his whole being was fired with a new emotion. Having no vocabulary he could not have described it had he wished. He only knew that every fibre of his body blazed with hate for those who threatened the wonderful creature he had been stalking—that something within urged him to her rescue, a something he could not resist.

With a low growl he sprang forward; and beside him leaped his tawny companion, the youth's fingers tangled in the black mane. The girl saw them coming and ceased her struggles—Allah was all-wise—He had furnished the means of escape from dishonor, and she was content even though it meant instant death.

"La il-ah-il-ah Allah. Mohammed ar-ra-sou-la Alah!" she breathed; and head held high, awaited her fate.

NINE

Count Maximilian Lomsk was in exile. He had been in exile for a year, ever since the night that King Otto had found him and Ferdinand and Hilda and the cobbler's pretty daughter in the hunting lodge. At present he was in Switzerland and without a great deal of money, for the count's father was rich only in blue blood and the amount of his debts. He was stopping at a cheap little hotel from which he had written many letters to Ferdinand begging him to intercede with his royal father to the end that Count Lomsk might return home; but Ferdinand never got the letters—Otto saw to that. Max guessed as much; so he had always written carefully to Ferdinand and spoken highly of the King, his father. His letters were really written quite as much for Otto as they were for Ferdinand; and because nothing came of them, Max's hatred of the King waxed.

At the same hotel was an elderly gentleman who looked like a college professor. He had arrived a week or so after Max. Max had paid no attention to him at first because he was elderly and because when the servants addressed him they called him only monsieur and not monsieur le conte or excellency or even doctor. Therefore Max assumed that he was a commoner and a nobody. In which, in a way, he was correct. But presently Max noticed that the elderly gentleman, seemingly accidentally and quite unostentatiously, revealed the fact that he possessed a rather large sum of money. After that Max became more interested in him. He even went as far as to say "Good morning" to him one day. That afternoon, as Max entered the bar, he saw the elderly gentleman sitting alone at a table. As Max approached, they both bowed; and as he was about to pass the table the elderly gentleman spoke to him.

"Will you do me the honor of sharing a bottle of wine with me?" he asked. "You seem to be as much alone and as lonely as I."

Max admitted that he would be delighted; and so he sat down and they shared several bottles of wine, the elderly gentleman doing the sharing and Max the drinking. They became very friendly; and as the wine loosened Max's tongue, he gave vent to the pent feelings to which he had not been able to unburden himself even in his letters to Ferdinand. The things that he said about King Otto that evening would make somebody's right ear burn.

They saw a great deal of each other every day after that; but Max was a little more careful what he said about King Otto after he learned that the elderly gentleman, who said his name was Kolchav, was a fellow countryman, until he discovered that Kolchav did not like Otto any better than he did. Kolchav was an excellent companion. He seemed to have plenty of money, and would not let Max pay for anything. He even loaned Max small amounts from time to time, and told him that he needn't mind about paying them back until it was perfectly convenient. Then, one evening, he said he was going back home the next day.

"Is there anything I can do for you back there?" he asked.

Max said he couldn't think of anything.

"Wouldn't you like to have me take a letter to Ferdinand?" asked Kolchav.

"Do you think you could get it to him?" asked Max.

"I am quite sure I could; and you may say anything you wish, for even if I were to read it, which I shall not, I should not divulge the contents. You might even put something in it for me."

"What is that?" asked Max.

"I should like to have a talk with Ferdinand," said Kolchav. "Perhaps if I were to talk with Ferdinand, we might find a way to get you back. You would be pretty well fixed, would you not, if you were back there and Ferdinand were king?"

"I should say I would," admitted Max. "I should have Sarnya's post if Ferdinand were king. He has promised it to me. I should be chief of staff, head of the army and the secret police."

"If Ferdinand were to promise that he would give the people such a constitution as they have demanded, an accident might befall the King. In that event, Ferdinand would succeed without opposition and with every guarantee that he would enjoy safety. It may not be easy to rid ourselves of Sarnya. He is very strongly intrenched; but eventually it can be done; and when it is, it shall be stipulated that you are to be chief of staff. All that you have to do is to give me a letter to Ferdinand, telling him that I am your good friend and his; and that he may trust me implicitly." Kolchav stopped and waited.

Max was suddenly a little frightened. "Who are you, Kolchav?" he demanded. "How do I know that you are not one of Sarnya's spies?"

"You don't know," Kolchav assured him, with a smile. "But I am not. I am only a simple old man who loves his country. However, if I were one of Sarnya's spies, you have already said enough to hang you several times over; so you might as well trust me. You will find me a good friend to have. I shall even arrange to have money sent to you regularly while you are in exile."

* * * *

The cobbler's pretty daughter had married a book-keeper who belonged to the revolutionary party of which Meyer was the patron saint, and who was so terrified at the thought of it that sometimes he could not sleep at night. He really was not at all the type that makes a successful revolutionist, and would have far better graced the Young Men's Christian Association or the Campfire Girls. He had other things to terrify him besides being a revolutionary. One was that Hilda de Groot and Crown Prince Ferdinand met at his home clandestinely; another was that the King might find it out. Altogether, William Wesl was a most unhappy benedict. He was about to be made more unhappy.

One evening, when he returned home from work, a mysterious stranger stepped up to him at his own door and thrust a message into his hand and disappeared around a corner into an alley. When William got inside the house he was afraid to open the letter. After he opened it behind a locked door in the inviolable seclusion of the toilet, he was frankly terrified, for even before he read the message he saw the signature at the bottom—a rough drawing of a dagger, the lower end of the blade of which had been significantly decorated with red ink. This was the symbol of the feared inner circle of the Revolutionary Party, grandiloquently known as The Terrorists. The message was short and to the point. It directed him to go to a certain corner at ten o'clock that night and follow a man whom he would find waiting there. William Wesl was not very good company for the cobbler's pretty daughter that evening at dinner or afterward. He seemed preoccupied, and when he announced that he would have to return to the office that evening, the cobbler's daughter became suspicious. She imagined several things, but principally blondes and brunettes; so there was a scene, and finally William had to tell her the truth; and then she was terrified, for she had known nothing of his connection with the revolutionists. Because of her relationship with Ferdinand and Maximillian, she was a staunch royalist; and as such she was terrified at the thought that her husband was a revolutionist. The full extent of the complications that might result were beyond her limited reasoning faculties, but she apprehended the worst.

At ten o'clock William found his guide at the appointed place and followed him through the dimly lighted streets of a poorer section of the city to a small inn, where he was conducted to a small back room and told to wait; then his guide departed. During the next few minutes Wesl lived a lifetime of agonizing apprehension. He could think of but one reason why The Terrorists wished to see him —they wanted him to assassinate some one. He was glad that no one knew that Ferdinand came to his home. It was fortunate that Ferdinand had been so very circumspect in the matter of his assignations. He had assured William that it was not possible for anyone to know that he visited the Wesl ménage. Perhaps they wanted him to assassinate the King! William shuddered, and he was still shuddering when an elderly gentleman entered the room and called him by name. This man did not look at all like a Terrorist—he looked more like a college professor.

"I have sent for you, Wesl," said Andresy, "because you or your wife sees Prince Ferdinand often."

William gulped and turned white. "It is nothing," he hastened to explain. "We cannot help it if he comes to our house. We do not want him to come."

"I understand," said Andresy. "I know all about it. He comes to meet the daughter of Martin de Groot, who was once chief gardener at the palace. Now what I want you to do is to get this letter to Ferdinand and bring me his reply. Do not give it to him yourself. Give it to your wife and have her give it to Hilda de Groot to give to Ferdinand. Neither woman must tell from whom she received the letter. Let each say that a stranger handed it to her on the street. Thus it will be impossible to trace it to me or to you if anything goes wrong. Let each woman understand that death will be the portion of the one who fails to observe these instructions. Ferdinand's reply must be handled similarly. Do you understand?"

"Yes, sir," said William, taking the letter.

* * * *

Crown Prince Ferdinand sat on the edge of General Count Sarnya's desk tapping his boot with a riding crop. He was visibly ill at ease. He hated Sarnya and had reason to suspect that Sarnya fully reciprocated his sentiments; so it was embarrassing to have to ask a favor of him. It was just another point to add to the score against Sarnya, the score that would be more than wiped out when Ferdinand became king.

"You recall the case of Lieutenant Carlyn, Count?" asked Ferdinand. "He was cashiered several years ago on account of some irregularity in the matter of a gambling debt, I think it was."

"I seem to recall it rather vaguely," replied Sarnya. "What about it?"

"Some of his fellow officers feel that an injustice was done him, and they have been importuning me to have him reinstated in the army. I have investigated the matter thoroughly, and I shall consider it a personal favor if you will see that he is returned to duty without loss of grades."

Now, Carlyn meant nothing to Sarnya; but he was glad of an opportunity to grant Ferdinand a favor, something that rarely occurred.

"I shall issue the necessary orders at once," he said.

* * * *

"Well," asked Carlyn as he entered the little back room where Andresy was enjoying a bottle of wine, "it has been some time since I saw you. Have you had any luck with the bad little boy of the palace?"

"Yes, I have seen him twice. He is absolutely ours. He has agreed to everything. I even believe that the dirty little louse would kill Otto himself to become king, if there was no other way. I saw him again last night after he had talked with Sarnya. The orders for your reinstatement without loss of grades has already been issued. That, of course, will take time. We must not arouse suspicion. Now, you must watch your step, Carlyn; no more marked cards or anything like that. You must be a model officer."

"You accuse me of cheating at cards?" demanded Carlyn angrily, springing to his feet.

"Sit down!" snapped Andresy. "Let us be honest with one another. You can't fool me; I know all about you, Carlyn. I think none the less of you because you are a card sharp and a trickster. It is well for the cause that I do know these things, otherwise I might trust you too far and not keep the careful watch on you that I do."

Carlyn sank back into his chair with a shrug. "Oh, well, what of it? I am not a cheat by choice. My mother bequeathed me extravagant tastes and my father left me no money."

TEN

It was the sudden rumbling growls of the lad and the lion that first attracted the attention of the marauders, all intent upon the struggle of their chief with the beautiful prisoner.

Turning, they beheld a sight that filled them with fear and consternation. There is little else on earth that an Arab fears as he fears a lion; and the sight of the prodigious proportions of the beast that was charging upon them was enough in itself to fill them with panic; but the presence of the naked white man, his face fierce with rage and hideous growls and roars bursting from his lips, was the last straw. Turning in every direction they sought their horses and escape; but several of the mounts, terrified at the roaring of the two beasts, had bolted up the canyon, and now three of the marauders, with their chief, found themselves at the mercy of the enemy.

The fellow who had grappled with Nakhla was so prostrated by fear that he still stood as one paralyzed, his fingers clutching the girl's arms, his head turned toward the charging demons, his eyes wide with terror. It was toward him that the youth leaped. To the lion he assigned the others—how, who may know? but as effectually as though the two owned a common language as good as yours and mine.

Nakhla, her level gaze full upon the youth, waited the outcome of his attack; and now the marauder, suddenly freed from the grip of his benumbing fright, released her and turned to meet the lad. There was no time to draw the long pistol from his belt, nor the keen knife—it was with naked hands alone that he must meet his unarmed foeman.

The lad, knowing no other method of attack than that which he had learned from the fierce carnivore, leaped straight for the Arab's throat, the weight of his body hurling the marauder to the ground. Rolling about among the bushes and the rocks the two battled with all the virgin ferocity of the primeval, for the son of the desert had advanced but little in the scale of humanity—he is the same today as he was when the first remote historian recorded his existence—and the lad was truly primal, as much so as the great cat he emulated.

Nakhla watched the battle with the keenest interest. A birthright of the daughters of the sun-stricken Sahara is an overwhelming admiration for physical supremacy in man, nor had this daughter of a sheik been denied a tithe or tittle of her dower. So engrossed was she in watching the strong, cat-like movements of the strange youth that she quite forgot to take advantage of the preoccupation of her enemies to escape. She saw that the lion had crushed with a single blow the head of one of the marauders and that after pursuing and dispatching another he had turned to the third, who was racing for his life toward some small trees that grew in the bottom of the canyon.

The fellow had had a good start; but the lion was covering the ground between them in huge bounds, his tail straight out behind, his jaws grinning wide, and savage roars thundering from his great lungs. It was a most impressive sight; but—after the marauders, what? The girl could not repress an involuntary shudder.

The man was within a few paces of the tree and safety, when, with a final mighty leap the lion sprang full upon

his back. The two rolled over and over to the very foot
of the tree that the man had hoped to reach. Then the
lion came to his feet. He was standing, his back toward
the girl, his legs wide apart straddling his victim, his head
down close to the head of the man. Nakhla saw a slight
movement of the massive head as the jaws closed. She
heard the crunching of bone. There was a sudden shaking
of the whole mighty frame, as of a terrier's when it shakes
a rat; then el adrea raised his dripping mouth to the
heavens and gave voice to the thundering challenge that
makes the earth tremble—the king of beasts had made
his kill.

So absorbed had the girl been for the moment in the
flight of the marauder and the lion's pursuit that she had
neglected the more important struggle going on so close
to her; but now her attention was suddenly recalled to it
by the sound of another mighty roar close behind her.

Another lion! She turned with startled alacrity to face
this new menace; but there was no lion. Instead, she saw
the youth standing over the body of the dead marauder
chief, and raising his voice to the heavens even as did
his savage companion.

Then it was that Nakhla realized the precious moments
she had thrown away, and what the neglect must cost
her. The youth was looking straight at her. In another
moment he would leap upon her as he had upon the
marauder, and she should feel those strong white teeth
at her throat. Then she saw his glance go past her, quickly,
and she turned to see what had attracted his attention.
She saw, and her knees went weak with the sight of it.
Not a dozen paces from her the great lion was trotting
toward her, his head and chin outstretched and flattened
low, his yellow-green eyes two menacing slits of cunning.

Instinctively Nakhla shrank toward the youth. He was

79

of human form—a man. Where else might intuition guide her for succor? It was the last scruple that was needed to tip the scales upon the side of humanity—the appeal of the woman for protection. Mute though it was it awoke a sleeping chord within the youth's broad breast—a chord that set his whole being vibrating in response.

With a quick, cat-like movement he stepped to her side, between her and the lion, and placing an arm about her called el adrea to his feet. What passed between the savage to the girl could not guess; but a moment later the lord of the wilderness rubbed his giant head against her knees; and then she felt the rasp of his rough tongue upon her hand, before he dropped, purring and contented, at her feet to lick the blood from his outstretched paws.

Nakhla turned, wide-eyed and wondering, to look up into the eyes of the youth. She found him gazing down upon her in equal wonder, and as their eyes met he smiled —such a gentle, manly, honest smile that won her confidence as no empty words might have done. She smiled back into his handsome face. His arm was still about her, nor did it seem strange to her that it should be so. A moment ago she had looked upon this man with feelings of terror, now it seemed that in all the world there was no other with whom she might be half so safe.

She tried to express the gratitude she felt for her rescue from the marauders, but it was soon evident to her that he understood no word of her language. His face took on a troubled expression as she talked, for he realized that she was attempting to communicate with him, though never before had he realized the possible existence of a spoken language.

Suddenly a new thought filled him with hope. He recalled the meager sign language that the old man of the derelict had taught him. Immediately his fingers commenced to fly before the girl's face; but to his disappointment he saw only as blank a look of incomprehension as her attempts at communication had brought to his own countenance. He gave up in despair.

Nakhla was at her wits end to find a way to explain to him that she wished to return to the safety of her father's douar. At last she tried taking him by the hand and leading him in the direction she wished to go, at the same time pointing up the canyon.

Finally he seemed to comprehend—the expression upon his face indicated it; but first he evidently had other matters to attend to. The sight of the dead marauders and the girl, all clothed as he had seen that the few others of his kind he had met always were had again aroused within him the desire for raiment.

He approached the body of the marauder chieftain, and after considerable study succeeded in removing the clothing; but his attempts to transfer it to his own person would have ended in failure had not Nakhla come to his rescue. With the aid of her nimble fingers the youth was soon clothed in the rags of the marauder. The belt and pistol as well as the long knife he appropriated, too, though he had no idea of the use of the firearm and but little as to that of the knife. However, his kind were thus equipped; and so it was his pride to be similarly dressed.

During the tedious ceremony of clothing his companion, the lion lay watching the proceeding with half-closed eyes. Whether he felt any misgivings of this first step of his friend in the direction of another life may not be known; but at least outwardly he ignored it nor ever did it change his attitude toward his young lord.

When the youth stood at last fully clothed he pointed up the canyon as the girl had pointed, and taking her by the hand led her in the direction she desired to go. The lion rose, yawning widely, and accompanied them, walking by Nakhla's side, so that she was between her two mighty protectors. She could not cease to wonder at the strange adventure that found her walking unafraid with the black mane of a great lion brushing her side.

When they had come to the steep ascent that leads over the hills at the canyon's end, the youth reached over and taking her left hand laid it upon the lion's mane, indicating to her that she should grasp it. At first she feared to do so; but the youth insisted, and presently she found herself clinging to the great beast and being drawn up the difficult ascent by him upon one side and the youth upon the other.

At the top, all breathless, they halted, and the girl and the man looked at one another and laughed. Nakhla was happy—she could not remember ever before having been so happy as she was that moment, standing there in the glare of the African sun looking out across the burning sands in the direction of the far douar of her tribe—close against her left side pressing the hot, fierce body of a lion, and upon the other a tall young white man whose fingers pressed her own slender brown ones in a clasp that seemed unwilling ever to release her. And furthest that moment from her mind was any thought of fear; though another emotion, all unknown to her, was knocking for admission there and to the unwon citadel of her virgin heart.

The youth, too, was happy. Happy with a great joy that surged through him—starting, to his wonderment, from the left hand that pressed the right hand of his lovely companion, and tingling on through every fibre of his being. So great was his happiness that he could not contain it—it must find vent in some form of physical expression. An ordinary man might have sung or shouted; but the youth was no ordinary man. Instead of singing, he raised his face to the wide, wide world and from his deep lungs there bellowed forth the roar of the lion who seeks his mate, and still the girl was unafraid. Upon her left the other savage beast raised his mighty voice in a similar thundering paean, and presently from afar off came the answering roar of a lioness.

A sudden, involuntary sigh burst from Nakhla's lips. Her fingers pressed those of the youth more closely. Her lithe young body leaned nearer to his; and as she raised her brown eyes to his grey, there was a puzzled, wondering question in them—an expression half of fear and half of hope. The lad, for with all his giant stature he was still but a lad, looked down into the eyes of the girl; and each read there in the other's that age-old, wordless poem whose infinite beauty and meaning neither as yet understood. They only knew that they were happy, and that it was good to be alive and together and that the world was a very wonderful place.

And then in silence, and hand in hand, with the great beast of prey beside them, they walked down into the desert setting their faces toward the east and the douar of Sheik Ali-Es-Hadji, for by now the youth understood their destination and that he was taking the girl back to her people.

It was quite dark by the time they came close to the tents. Here they halted a hundred yards from the douar. The girl tried gently to lead the man on with her to her father's tent that the old sheik might thank him who had saved her from a fate worse than death; but the youth was timid with the timidity of the wild thing in the face of the habitations of men. That he was not afraid the girl knew. Instinctively she guessed the truth; and then she commenced to wonder if he would let her go to her people, for she had not been ignorant entirely of the meaning of the pressure upon her hand or the light in the eyes of her companion. She was as pure as he, but her life among human beings had resulted in a certain sophistication that was still unknown to the lad.

When she tried to say goodbye to him he seemed to understand; and he let her go, for in his heart he knew that he should see her again; and in her eyes, even in the moonlight, he read the wish that it should be so. And so, with a pressure of the hands, she left him standing there under the brilliant moon upon the yellow sands, the great lion at his side, and about the lion's neck one of his strong, tanned arms showing beneath the back flung burnoose of the dead marauder chieftain.

At the edge of the tents she flung a backward, longing glance, to see the two silent figures still standing as she had left them—the lad and the lion, into whose lives had come a new power, greater than any with which they had ever coped—greater than their lifelong friendship—more potent than the mighty thews of steel that rolled so softly beneath their savage skins.

The girl raised her hand above her head and waved a farewell to the man. He answered her in kind, his heart leaping at the sight of her. And then she was gone within the tents of her people.

From far out across the moon-bathed sands came, faintly, the roar of a lioness. The beast beneath the man's hand thrilled and trembled; and then from his fierce throat broke an answering roar.

ELEVEN

The king sat scowling at the Crown Prince; but that was nothing unusual, as the King always scowled, only he scowled most at Ferdinand.

"You are twenty-one," he said. "It is time you were marrying. I have arranged for you to go to the father's capital and ask for the hand of the Princess Maria."

"I do not want to marry yet," said Ferdinand. "I do not want to marry Maria at all. She has a long face and buck teeth. I can never decide whether she looks more like a horse or a rabbit."

"It makes no difference what you want or what she looks like," snapped Otto; "you are going to marry her. I command it. You still have the little Dutch girl——"

"Who says that?" demanded Ferdinand. "It's a lie."

King Otto sneered. "You were not bright enough to fool Sarnya," he said. "He can tell you every time you have met the girl and where."

"Damn Sarnya!" snapped Ferdinand. "When I am king, I'll——"

"When you are king, if you ever are, you'll do well to make your peace with Sarnya and do what he tells you to do, like a good boy. He is all that stands between the throne and revolution—all that stands between us and The Terrorists—and Death. I don't like him myself—he shows too little respect for my position—but I know when I am well off."

"It is too bad that that man Bulvik was such a poor shot," said Ferdinand.

"If he had been a better shot it might have been our

turn next," said the King, "and you wouldn't have had to marry the Princess Maria. The arrangements have all been made for you to visit her father the first of the month. You will have a good time, and you can thank Bulvik's poor aim."

* * * *

Hans de Groot had graduated from The Royal Military Academy, and was now a second lieutenant of cavalry. His regiment was stationed along the frontier, strung out in isolated posts with only a few men and an officer to a post. Their duties consisted mostly of preventing contraband goods and political undesirables from crossing the border. The assignment was monotonous; Hans found it hateful. He wished that he might be stationed in the capital. He often mentioned this in his letters home to his father and mother. He never wrote to Hilda nor mentioned her in any of his letters. Sometimes his mother said Hilda was well and sent her love, but his father never mentioned Hilda either.

Martin de Groot had a nursery on the outskirts of the city. He was far more prosperous than when he had been working as head gardener for the King. When people saw Hilda come home for a visit with her mother, as she occasionally did when her father was away, they would have thought Martin de Groot must be making a great deal of money; for Hilda rode in a beautiful English car with a chauffeur and footman. She wore expensive clothes, and in the winter time her furs were the envy of the capital.

The neat little cottage where Martin and his wife lived was too small and too far from the center of the capital to suit Hilda; so, for these and other reasons, she lived in an expensive apartment a few blocks from the palace. One day, when Ferdinand dropped in for cocktails, Hilda chanced to be alone. She had come in just ahead of him and still had on her hat and wraps. Ferdinand asked her where she had been.

"I have been visiting Mother," she said. "I saw a letter from Hans. He does not like it on the frontier. He said he wished he could be transferred to another regiment—one stationed here in the capital. He would like to be near Mother and Father; and they would like to have him, for they are very much alone now. You will do that for me, dear, won't you?"

"Hans does not like me very well," said Ferdinand. "Do you think it would be safe to have him here? I had him sent to the frontier because I thought it would be safer for both of us."

"Oh, Hans is a man now," said Hilda. "He will look at things differently, and when I tell him that we are going to be married as soon as you are king everything will be all right."

Ferdinand looked very uncomfortable. He lit a cigarette and threw it away; then he drank a cocktail at a single gulp and lighted another cigarette.

"I don't know that everything is going to be all right," he said. "I have some bad news."

"Bad news? What is it?" demanded Hilda.

"The King wants me to marry."

"Whom?"

"The Princess Maria."

"I don't believe he wants you to marry her," sobbed Hilda. "You love her. You are tired of me."

"Love that horse-faced scarecrow! Don't be silly. I don't love anyone but you. I never have and never shall," and that was the truth. It was one of the few decent things about Ferdinand.

"Then if you loved me, you'd marry me—you wouldn't marry her."

"Oh, for heaven's sake, Hilda! Can't you understand that I have nothing to do with it? The King has commanded that I marry her. As soon as I'm king, I'll divorce her and marry you. Nobody can stop me."

"I won't have you; I won't ever see you again, if you marry her," sobbed Hilda. "You could do something about it if you cared."

Do something about it! Ferdinand sat staring at the carpet, his eyes wide as though he were frightened, his fingers twitching. Do something about it!

* * * *

"It is quite difficult getting here or anywhere else unobserved," said Carlyn. "Sarnya's people are everywhere."

"You probably imagine that," suggested Andresy, "because you have a guilty conscience."

"Perhaps," agreed Carlyn. "However, I feel that we should not attempt it again until——"

"Yes, you are right. However, I did want to see you. There are several things we should discuss. How are you progressing?"

"Exceptionally well; but first tell me about your trip to Switzerland. Did you accomplish anything?"

"Very little," replied Andresy. "Lomsk is not trustworthy. He is also a coward; and he is actuated by his desire to satisfy his greed and his vanity, both of which are inordinate. He would do anything for money. He would betray us or Ferdinand as quickly as he would Otto, if the price were right. But to be General Count Lomsk, Chief of Staff, he would sell his soul; and not for any constructive purpose, either—just to wear the epaulets and strut before the ladies. He might have done something for us in Switzerland by consolidating the expatriates there and in France, but all he did was to spend the money we have been sending him on a blonde from Germany. However, we shall have to put up with him. He will be a power behind the throne when Ferdinand is king. And now, tell me how things have been going with you. Are you any closer to the palace?"

"I am practically in it," replied Carlyn. "Within a day or two I am to be transferred to The Guards. I don't know how Ferdinand accomplished it, unless it is that Sarnya is attempting to keep peace in the family by granting unimportant favors to Ferdinand—what Sarnya thinks are unimportant. Once in The Guards, some day I shall be Officer of the Guard inside the palace. It will be an ordinary, routine detail. That, my good friend Andresy, will be *the* day!"

"Let us drink to it," said Andresy, raising his glass.

"I have another matter to report that may be important and may not," continued Carlyn. "It has possibilities, however; and I shall continue to follow it up."

"Yes? and what is it?"

"Recently a young lieutenant was transferred from the frontier to my regiment here. He is the brother of Hilda de Groot. When I found that out, I cultivated him, you may be sure. He is a very fine young man. I made it a point to take him under my wing, and now we are the best of friends. As I suspected, he hates Ferdinand."

"Good!" exclaimed Andresy. "It is well to be prepared for any eventuality, especially in this instance, as I am quite sure that Ferdinand is going to make a very bad king who will want his own way—a mistake that the more experienced kings have recently learned to avoid."

"Now," said Carlyn, "as I may not be able to see you again before The Day, I should like to explain exactly what I wish done when I sent you the word. I have worked it all out very carefully. Please do not ask any questions—just trust me. I shall be gambling my life, you know."

"I would like to place a bet that you do not lose it," said Andresy, with a smile.

"I do not intend losing it," Carlyn assured him. "Now listen carefully."

* * * *

Lieutenant Hans de Groot dropped into the little cottage on the outskirts of the capital one afternoon for a short visit with his mother and father, but neither one of them was there. The maid-of-all work told him that the latter was away on a job and that his mother was out shopping but would be back soon.

While Hans was waiting in the little parlor, a limousine stopped at the curb, a liveried footman sprang out and opened the door, and Hilda de Groot stepped from the tonneau. She did not know that Hans was in the cottage; and Hans, who was reading a magazine, had not heard the quiet motor as it pulled up and stopped. He heard the front door open and close; and when he looked up, Hilda was standing in the doorway of the parlor. It was the first time they had seen one another since that fateful night four years before when Hans had waited in the garden to kill Ferdinand. Hilda was now a beautiful young woman, from whose pulchritude the art of Molyneaux had certainly detracted nothing. Hans came slowly to his feet. His face was stern and uncompromising. The girl's great beauty struck him almost as a blow in the face. To him, it was the hallmark of her shame, of the disgrace she had brought upon the family.

Hilda flushed. "Oh, Hans!" she breathed. "It is so good to see you. Please do not be cross. Why can you not understand?"

"Understand! What is there to understand that all the world does not know?"

"If you knew anything of love, you would understand —and forgive."

"Love!" He spit the word out.

"It is love," she said, simply. "We love each other so much."

"And because he loves you so much, he has gone away to ask another woman to marry him!"

"That is not his fault," the girl defended. "The King commanded it, but Ferdinand will never marry her. He has promised me that he will not; and when he is king, he will marry me."

"And you believe that?"

"Absolutely."

"Then I am sorry for you because you are such a fool. He will never marry you. He has no intention of marrying you; and even if he had, they would never permit it. Do you think the nobles, the army, or the people would accept a Dutch gardener's daughter as queen?"

"Stranger things than that have happened," she replied; "even swineherds have become kings. When Ferdinand is king, he will *be* king; then he will do as he pleases. He is not afraid of them."

"I shall wait and see what he does when he is king," said Hans.

TWELVE

Even as Nakhla entered the tent of her father she realized the folly of attempting to convince her people of the truth of her day's experiences. They would never believe her. So she decided that reference to the lad and the lion had better be left unmade.

Her father and his people were wild with joy at her safe return, and to account for her absence she told of her capture by the marauders and her eventual escape.

El Djebel, her horse, had not yet returned. A party of young tribesmen were scouring the desert for her, but they had gone to the east instead of the west. They returned late the following morning, and an hour later El Djebel wandered unconcernedly into the camp in search of food and water.

For several days Nakhla found no opportunity to leave camp unattended though she longed to go out into the hills in search of her strange new friends. Her mind was occupied with nothing else than thoughts of the tall and noble youth whose eyes had drunk deep from the depths of her own. She made Ben Saada sick with the torture of her indifference, until, finally, goaded to desperation, he went to her father, demanding the hand of Nakhla in marriage.

Twenty camels offered Ben Saada for the daughter of Sheik Ali-Es-Hadji; but the old sheik told him that he must win Nakhla's consent first, for Ali-Es-Hadji was already rich, as riches go within the desert, and Nakhla was his only daughter. So Ben Saada went to Nakhla, laying his heart at her feet; but still was the girl obdurate; so that the man, from pleading, fell to threatening, whereat her head went high and she turned her back upon him.

Beneath Ben Saada's dark skin beat a darker heart. The man thought that he loved the maid, but within the breast of such as Ben Saada could burn no unselfish flame. Really, at the bottom of his passion was only base desire and ambition, for Sheik-Ali-Es-Hadji was without a son; and Ben Saada saw himself as the son-in-law of the old sheik, a sheik himself upon the death of Ali-Es-Hadji.

There was a way to bring the girl to time, and that way Ben Saada swore that he would take the moment that opportunity presented. In the meantime he could wait, and scowling beneath the hood of his burnoose he strode away to his goatskin tent.

For a week the lad, far out in the hills, roamed and hunted by himself; for the lion had answered the call of the lioness, and now only occasionally did he return to the rocky lair upon the hillside. The youth, proud in his new apparel, strutted about like a peacock; but when it came to hunting he discovered that his finery was much in his way. The dirty white burnoose attracted the attention of his quarry long before he came within striking distance; and it was soon clear to him that he must abandon, temporarily, either his clothing or his food.

Naturally he chose the former alternative. Rolling his garments into a dank and sweaty wad he hid them in the darkest corner of his den. Then he went out to fall upon an unwary antelope as it watered at the brook. The knife he carried, for its practical usefulness had been readily apparent to him from the first. He wore it in the Arab's belt about his naked waist, and found it simplified the matter of feeding upon the flesh of his kill. Heretofore he had torn away great mouthfuls with his strong, white teeth; but now, with the knife, he found it much easier to cut strips from the carcass.

Carrying the dead antelope to the ledge before his lair he feasted to repletion. Then he donned his clothes once more, and lay down to sleep after the manner of wild beasts that have filled their bellies; but he found that sleep would not come. His mind was a riot of thoughts and memories, for he was a man. Had he been a lion, it would have been different.

He saw the beautiful face of the girl he had left outside the tents of her people a few nights before. He had daily hoped that she would come again to his valley. His timidity had kept him from approaching her camp by day, though nearly every night had found him wandering close to the tents of the tribe of Ali-Es-Hadji; but never had he seen the girl, though once, early in the evening, he had thought that he heard her voice.

At last he arose from his rock bed. He would go out into the edge of the desert and look for her—possibly she would come this day. He moved quickly along the bottom of the canyon, upward toward the pass. At the hilltop he paused to look out across the sands toward the cluster of date palms and the tents of the people of Nakhla. They were but a single tiny splotch of green, far, far away upon the desert; yet at sight of them his heart beat faster and a great joy welled within his breast.

Now he saw something moving between him and the oasis—a little speck of darker sand upon the yellow. Motionless as a statue stood the youth—the training of the carnivore apparent in the narrowed lids and the blazing eyes and in the half crouch of his giant body. Like a shadow he melted behind a nearby bush, so gradual his movement that it could scarce have attracted the eye of one nearby.

From his hiding place he watched that which moved upon the desert. It was approaching. Presently he saw that it was one upon a horse, and when it had reached the first ascent from the desert to the hills the youth leaped from his hiding place and ran swiftly to meet it.

It was Nakhla. At sight of the man running toward her she drew rein, for she did not know yet that it was he; but when she heard the rumbling roar of a lion tumble from his lips she spurred on her trembling mount, pressing upward to meet him.

All the way from her father's douar she had told herself over and over again that she but rode today for the pleasure of riding, that she neither expected nor hoped to meet anyone upon the way, and least of all a white stranger who was more beast than human and who, in addition, was doubtless a Nasrâny—hated of her people —dog of an unbeliever.

Nakhla had worked herself into quite a heat of self-righteous indignation that anyone should dare to ascribe to her such an unthinkable motive when she chanced to glance again toward the summit of the hills she was approaching and there saw a man running toward her. At first her heart had stood quite still, until the savage roar of welcome rolling down upon her ears had set it to beating wildly; and then forgetting all but the man before her she spurred El Djebel upward toward him.

At his side she drew rein, timid and afraid now that she was come into his presence. He took her hand and stroked it, for he knew no form of greeting such as men use. For years he had stroked the tawny coat of the lion as the only outward manifestation of affection for his one friend; so it was not strange that he should stroke the cool and shapely hand of Nakhla, his new friend, who awakened within his savage and untutored breast a chaos of pleasurable emotions.

The girl slipped from El Djebel to stand at his side, and looking up into his face she spoke to him; but he only shook his head sadly, for he could not understand. And then there came to her a sudden determination— she would teach this stranger who sent the blood coursing madly through her veins the language of her people, for

she longed to hear him voice the sentiments that his eyes
and his stroking hand proclaimed.

She was at a loss as to just how she might commence
her task until it occurred to her that she would like to
hear her own name upon his lips. Yes, that should be the
first word that he should speak; and so, pointing to herself, she repeated, "Nakhla" several times over.

He understood at once, and smiling, repeated the word
after her. Laughing, the girl clapped her brown hands. He
had said it! He had spoken her name, nor had it ever
sounded quite the same to her before as it did from the
firm lips of this Nasrâny.

Then she pointed to El Djebel, saying in Arabic,
"Horse," and the man repeated, "Horse." Thus she continued her first lesson, pointing out all the familiar ob-
jests about them until he could name each accurately in
the language of his tutor. He learned quickly, for his mind
was unspoiled, and he had nothing to unlearn.

As they talked, the youth, holding one of her hands,
led her back down into his own rocky little canyon,
where, beside a spreading palm, they sat together by the
brook's brim looking into each other's eyes while the man
recited his lesson.

Nakhla was very proud of her success as a teacher. It
would not be long, at this rate, before the man could talk
to her—and tell her what was in his heart. The same
thought filled the mind of the youth, so that when the girl
paused for a moment he pointed out new objects questioningly, nor did he once confuse the names of any, or
make a single error after she had taught him the correct
pronunciation.

He prefaced everything with "Nakhla" to attract her
attention; and then he would point to the thing the name
of which he wished to learn. His mind was fertile and

resourceful. He found many ways to learn, since he had commenced, that the girl would never have thought of. Pointing to his feet he learned how to call them in Arabic, and then rising he walked still pointing to his feet, and she, understanding, taught him the verb, to walk. Then he ran, learning the verb.

He stood, and sat, and lay down. He climbed a tree. He drank from the brook. He did the many, little every-day things that were most familiar to him; and as he learned the nouns and verbs, unconsciously he learned, too, the articles, prepositions and conjunctions, from the constant repetition of them upon Nakhla's lips as she spoke to him while he was learning.

At last the girl realized that it was growing late, and that she must return to her father's douar. She made the youth understand, and together they took their way across the hills to the desert. Here she mounted El Djebel, but the man would not let her ride alone across the wilderness. With a hand upon her stirrup leather he ran beside her, keeping pace with the galloping horse with as little apparent effort as the horse himself, for the lad and the lion had often run great distances in pursuit of their prey, frequently across rough and rugged country, so that this was but child's play for his mighty muscles.

When they had come as close to the camp as Nakhla dared venture with her strange companion she reined in El Djebel, and leaning down close to the youth whispered her goodbye. He repeated the words after her, though he did not as yet comprehend their import.

However, the new words awakened a new thought in the man's mind. He had learned the names of many things that day, but there was one as yet who remained nameless. He pointed to the girl, saying, "Nakhla" and then he pointed to himself, questioningly.

Nakhla laughed, a puzzled expression contracting her finely penciled brows. In her mind he was "The Man," but that was no name for him. She must find another. For a moment the girl racked her brain for a suitable cognomen. Then as one swept into her mind she flushed and hesitated, scarce daring to voice it aloud.

But the youth was insistent. He kept pointing to himself. Asking with his eyes as clearly as though his lips had spoke for a word whereby he might be called.

At last, leaning from her saddle, Nakhla placed a cool palm upon his forehead with a tenderness that was unmistakably a caress. Close to his ear came her lips, and a sudden flush mantled her cheeks.

"Azîz," she whispered. "Thou are Nakhla's azîz," and then she was away as fast as El Djebel could bear her.

Enveloped in a little cloud of sand, he saw her disappear within the douar, but not before she had turned to wave him an adieu.

"Azîz!" repeated the youth aloud. "Azîz!" And he thought it a fine name. Had he guessed its meaning he would have liked it no less.

For a long time he stood gazing at the tents of her people. He wondered why it was that he alone of all the other creatures of his kind should have been doomed to solitude. He heard the hum of human voices and an occasional laugh and, after the moon had risen, strains of melody from the primitive musical instruments of the tribe. He tried to discover the sweet notes of Nakhla's voice among the others, and when he thought that he had succeeded the lure of it drew him closer to the tents, until at last he stood close within their shadow—a silent statue of untutored savagery, whose fallow heart and soul, ready for the seeding of good or evil which contact with humanity must bring, lay wholly in the keeping of a half-savage maid.

As he stood listening within the douar, the talking and the music within gradually diminished until at last silence fell upon the camp, and with the release of his faculties from the enchantment that the hope of hearing her voice had cast upon them, he became aware of the scent of goats and camels, and with it he felt the gnawing of hunger at his belly.

Slowly and cautiously he moved around the tents that he might come close to the barrier that penned the flocks. At the same moment Nakhla, sleepless from much thinking of her Azîz, came out into the moonlight before her father's tent. As she stood idly gazing through half-closed eyes, recalling the face and figure of her savage giant, she saw a sudden apparition appear for an instant as it leaped the wall of the corral in among the animals of her tribe.

Instantly she knew who it must be, and running swiftly she came to the gate that led into the enclosure where the herd was kept. Even as she pushed through the gate she heard the frightened bleat of a kid, and then she was within and close before her saw the man of her dreams with his strong fingers about the neck of one of the flock.

He saw her at the instant that she entered, and forgetful of his hunger dropped his prey and came quickly to her side. Gently Nakhla laid her hand upon his arm, and pointing to the kid upon the ground and to the other animals within the enclosure she tried to tell him that he must not harm them. Waving a hand back toward the tents she imitated the position of a man firing a gun, pointing the imaginary weapon at him. He understood this last, but he only laughed and shrugged his shoulders. She saw that he was not one to be influenced by threat of personal danger.

Then she tried a new plan, and indicating herself attempted to make him understand that for her sake he must not tamper with the animals of her people. And this he comprehended, for love is not so blind as some would have us believe. He was very hungry; and for a moment he looked ruefully toward the kid that by now had struggled to its feet and was wobbling back into the herd, but a new force had come into his life—it was no longer to be his belly that dominated all his acts, and thus he took a great stride toward humanness as he turned silently away and with an agile bound cleared the barrier to disappear from Nakhla's sight.

After he had gone she would have recalled him, for she thought that he was hurt; and then she wondered if he had not really been hungry! The idea filled her with dismay. She had driven her Azîz out into the desert when he had come friendless and hungry in search of food.

Nakhla did not sleep much that night for the self-reproach that gnawed at her heart; but she might have saved herself her misery, for the object of her solicitude felt only happiness that he had found a way to please the girl who had come into his lonely life. Never again, he told himself, would he or the lion despoil the flocks of her people.

Across the lonely desert he made his way toward the distant hills where the lair was, and all the long way his heart sang within his breast so loudly that it drowned the demands of hunger. Nor did he again think of eating until he had come almost to the entrance of his den when the reek of blood filled his nostrils; and suddenly in the moonlight upon the ledge he saw a fresh-killed antelope and upon it a strange lioness that arose, growling horribly, at his approach.

THIRTEEN

The Princess Maria's father was one of the richest monarchs in Europe, in his own right. His kingdom was prosperous, too; but his people were not particularly warlike. They seemed to prefer hoes in their hands to bayonets in their bellies. Some people are like that, and it is always a matter of embarrassment to their rulers. Ferdinand's father, on the other hand, was poor; and his country in debt. His people were overtaxed; but they liked to goosestep and salute; and while they didn't particularly relish having bayonets poked into them, they were willing to take a chance for the sake of having an opportunity of poking their bayonets into other people. An alliance of the two houses, therefore, would give each what it lacked and wished.

In the capital of the Princess Maria's father, Ferdinand was wined and dined and banqueted and feted for a week. His entertainment was lavish and expensive. Nothing was left undone that might impress upon him the prosperity and wealth of his host and his host's country, and Ferdinand was impressed. For the first time he commenced to see the possibilities of the alliance. There were royal yachts and royal trains and royal other things that were far more royal than anything Ferdinand had ever seen before. He tried to forget that Maria was horsefaced and bucktoothed. He also tried to forget a certain promise he had made to Hilda de Groot.

The night before he was to leave for home, he found himself alone with Maria on a moon-bathed terrace. She didn't look quite so badly by moonlight, but he couldn't help thinking that she would have looked less badly had there been no moon. She was a difficult person to whom to make love—she was rather ugly, she was three years older than he, and she was all bones. However, it had to be done. Ferdinand took a deep breath and steeled himself, as one who is about to dive into very cold water. Finally he took the plunge.

"I have the honor," he said, "to ask your hand in marriage."

* * * *

King Otto was far more contented than he had been for years. His son was to marry the daughter of his very rich neighbor. Otto was almost happy, for the world looked quite bright.

"The treaty," he said to Sarnya; "it should be signed at once."

"They will not sign it until after the marriage has taken place," replied Sarnya.

"And the loan?" asked Otto.

"That must wait, too."

"But why?" demanded the King.

"If they made the loan, it would strengthen us materially, for they know that most of it is to be spent on armament. They want Maria's influence with Ferdinand as assurance that we won't use that armament against them. Their attitude is quite correct. We should do the same under like circumstances. You must remember that in the last one hundred years we have made war on them twenty times and broken every treaty that we have signed. You can't blame them. They are banking heavily on Maria."

"Too heavily, I am afraid," said Otto.

"Why do you say that?" asked Sarnya.

"She will exercise no influence over Ferdinand. The chances are that she won't see him much more than once a month after they are married. There is still the Dutch girl."

"She can be gotten rid of," suggested Sarnya. "Give her a little money and send her out of the country."

"It wouldn't work," said Otto. "The fool is in love with her. He'd follow her. Why, he even wanted to marry her."

"There are other ways of getting rid of her—permanently," said Sarnya.

Otto shook his head. "Only as a last resort," he said. "It will be better if Ferdinand has her for diversion. I can imagine that a man might get rather desperate if he had to depend solely on Maria for entertainment."

* * * *

"You have been back three whole days, and this is the first time you have come to see me."

"I have been very busy," explained Ferdinand.

"That is not the reason. You did not come to see me because you are ashamed. The papers say that you are to marry Maria next month. I know now that you are; otherwise you would not have been ashamed to come and see me."

"It is not my fault, Hilda. If I were king, it would be different; but I am not king."

"You went there, and you found that you loved her. If you didn't love her, you wouldn't be in such a hurry to marry her."

"I am in no hurry to marry her. I do not want to marry her at all. You do not understand. The marriage is a matter of State. There is a treaty to be signed that will be very advantageous to our country, but it will not be signed until after I have married Maria."

"Then you are going to marry her?"

"I can't help it. I have to."

"You told me you would never marry anyone but me."

"I don't want to marry anyone but you, Hilda. I am doing this for my country. Later, I can divorce her and marry you."

"Another one of your promises. I shall go away and enter a convent. You shall never see me again." Hilda began to cry.

"Don't do that," he snapped, irritably. "How much do you think I can stand? It is bad enough to have to marry a clotheshorse with buckteeth, without having you reproach me and make a scene."

"I am not making a scene. When one's heart is broken, can one help crying? I shall probably die. I want to die."

"You will not die; and if you will be patient, maybe something will happen so that I shall not have to marry Maria."

"What could happen?" demanded Hilda.

"Oh, one never knows," said Ferdinand.

* * * *

The great day arrived, and nothing happened. Maria's father had come and her mother and a horde of other relatives in addition to the King's entourage. The capital was gay with flags and bunting, the avenues were lined with soldiers, the air was filled with military planes. The escort included cavalry, infantry, tanks, anti-aircraft guns, armored cars, and even heavy field pieces; for Otto was trying to impress Ferdinand's future father-in-law with his wealth of men and armament, just as the latter had sought to impress Ferdinand with his display of wealth.

Crowds lined the avenue of the cathedral. They waved flags and cheered dutifully. William Wesl and the cobbler's pretty daughter were among them. William did not wave

a flag or cheer. He wore a heavy scowl. That was because
he was a revolutionary, and revolutionaries always scowl.
The cobbler's daughter, however, was very enthusiastic.
She waved her little flag and shouted and clapped her
little hands, which caused her to drop the flag; and when
William stooped to retrieve it, someone bumped him in
the seat, so that he nearly sprawled on his face, which
did nothing toward improving William's disposition. That
was so bad this bright and sunny morning that William
almost felt that he should like to be a Terrorist. He was
trying to compute, roughly, what all this was going to
cost the taxpayers; and that didn't make him feel any
better, either; for he could see that it was going to cost
a great deal. Maria would cost them a lot, too; and then
there would be children, and there would be further demands on the taxpayers. The future looked black to William.

Hilda de Groot did not watch the procession; she lay
face down on her bed, sobbing.

Andresy watched the procession; but, notwithstanding
the fact that he also was a revolutionary, he smiled; for
he knew that The Day was approaching. A young lieutenant sitting on his horse in front of his troop, his sword
at salute, watched Ferdinand roll past in a gilded coach.
It was as well for Ferdinand's peace of mind that he did
not know what was in this young lieutenant's mind. In
Switzerland, Count Maximilian Lomsk listened to the
broadcast of all the ceremonies attendant upon the marriage of a crown prince to a princess. A little blonde from
Germany sat beside him.

"When Ferdinand is king and recalls me from exile,"
he told her, "I shall send for you. I shall be a very great
man, then; and you shall live as befits the friend of a
great man." Once he had told the cobbler's pretty daugh-

ter something along the same general line, but he had forgotten that, along with the cobbler's pretty daughter.

Resplendent in his Guard uniform, Captain Carlyn watched King Otto pass; and licked his dry lips.

* * * *

Hilda de Groot was writing in her diary a few days after the marriage of Ferdinand and Maria, when a man burst into her boudoir without being announced or without knocking. That is, he had not knocked on her door; but he had knocked her butler down, and had run upstairs so fast that he had almost knocked her maid off the landing as he brushed past her.

"Where is he?" he demanded, as he burst into the room, a drawn revolver in his hand.

"Hans!" cried Hilda. "What is the matter? Have you gone mad?"

"Where is he?" repeated Hans, looking about the boudoir.

"Where is who?"

"You know—that rat, that pig—Ferdinand."

"He is not there. I have not seen him since—since he was married." She was staring at the revolver, horrified. "Hans! What did you intend doing? You must have gone crazy even to think of such a thing. What good would it do? What is done, is done; and why should you want to kill the man I love? Do you think I am not unhappy enough as it is? Would you make it worse? They would shoot you, Hans; and I love you, too. Think what it would do to Mamma and Papa. It might kill them."

He sank into a chair. "Yes," he said, "I guess I have gone a little crazy. But who wouldn't? I have thought of nothing else for more than five years. Every night of my life I have killed him—sometimes one way, sometimes another. We used to be so happy, Hilda, you and I and

Michael; and then he came along, and everything was spoiled. Why shouldn't I hate him? Why shouldn't I want to kill him?"

"Because I love him."

He shook his head, as though to clear something from his brain; then he rose slowly to his feet. "I am glad I did not find him here," he said. "Perhaps you are right. I shall try to remember; but sometimes this hate engulfs me like a great wave, and then I can think only of one thing—to kill, to kill him and you."

"Hans!" she cried, horrified.

"I cannot help it," he said. "I do not want to kill you. I do not want to want to kill you. Oh, I wish that I were dead."

He walked slowly from the room, then. Hilda noticed that he walked almost like an old man; then she threw herself face down upon the floor, and sobbed.

FOURTEEN

The growling of the lioness brought the youth to a sudden halt, and it also brought another actor into the little drama—the black-maned beauty, who after his savage fashion loved them both.

As the lioness rose to charge the youth the lion leaped quickly in front of her, and approaching his human friend rubbed his muzzle against him, purring an affectionate greeting. Then he turned back toward the lioness as though to say: "You see, do you not, that this is my friend? I do not harm him, nor must you."

The lioness looked her puzzlement, and with much

grumbling resumed her repast; but the youth was hungry, and though he knew that he took his life in his hands he pushed forward to the kill. Again the lioness came to her feet, mouthing her hideous warning with upcurled lips and bared fangs. The youth ignored her. The lion stood almost between them. The man drew his knife and cut a strip from the kill. The lioness took a step forward him, but her mate shoved his mighty shoulder between them. Then the lioness turned away and fell to eating, while the youth squatted upon his haunches at the opposite end of the carcass and filled his belly.

When the meal was done he drawled into the den, and a moment later the two great beasts crawled in beside him and lay down. It was very dark within the den. The youth could not see the forms of his companions; but he heard their breathing, and his last waking memory was of the two blazing eyes of the lioness glaring at him through the darkness. Then he slept.

The next morning the lioness seemed to accept the presence of the youth as a matter of no moment. He moved about with the two as though he had been a third lion, and when he brushed against the great female she paid no more attention to him than she did to her savage mate.

But with all that he was in no danger from the great beasts he no longer felt as he had when he and the lion had been the sole possesors of each other's friendship. Now he was an outsider, and the longer he thought upon it the more he craved the companionship of the girl of the tented village.

He went, now, daily down into the desert; and Nakhla came daily to meet him. His education proceeded rapidly, for he was as anxious to learn as she was to teach;

and as he grasped sufficient of the rudiments of her language to enable him to ask questions he made progress that was astonishing.

Thus a month passed, the youth lairing with the two lions, feeding upon their kills and assisting them in their hunting. The lioness had grown attached to him, coming to his side for caresses as did the great lion; so that it was no uncommon sight for the beasts of the hills to see the three basking in the sun by the riverside; the youth lying with an arm about the neck of the great lion, while the lioness lay with her chin across the man's breast or rubbed her cool muzzle against his bronzed neck and cheek.

Yet always was the youth impatient for the time that he might live within the tents of the Sheik Ali-Es-Hadji, for Nakhla had promised that one day, when he spoke the language of her people fluently, she should take him to her father and ask that he be accepted as one of the tribe. It was Nakhla who taught him to ride and to shoot, for the girl realized that his position would be sufficiently difficult among her savage tribesmen without the handicap of unfamiliarity with the accomplishments they held most dear.

Now Ben Saada during all this time had not remained inactive. He was not long in comprehending that the girl's affections were not for him, and jealousy prompted him to suspect that they were directed toward another. So he watched Nakhla surreptitiously, and once he followed her during one of her daily solitary rides which had finally confirmed his suspicion that the sheik's daughter had found a lover outside the douar of her father.

He saw Nakhla meet a white-robed figure far out upon the desert and the two sit together for hours laughing and talking; and though he witnessed no outward manifestations of love between them, yet he knew that only love could draw the daughter of the sheik daily to meet this stranger.

Upon his return to camp he lost no time in warning Ali-Es-Hadji, and when the latter seemed inclined to doubt his story he promised to take him the following day to the trysting place of the lovers.

And thus it came about that upon the day following Sheik Ali-Es-Hadji's trip into the desert with Ben Saada, Azîz found no Nakhla at the meeting place, nor on the next day nor the next; and though he went each evening close to the tents of her people he saw nothing of her.

Upon the fourth day as he approached the place where they had been accustomed to meet he saw a solitary white-robbed horseman where he had hoped to find Nakhla. At the sight of Azîz the Arab made the sign of peace, and when the youth was close to him addressed him.

"I come from Nakhla, daughter of Sheik Ali-Es-Hadji," said the horseman. "She wished me to find you and tell you that she may come no more into the desert, for yesterday she was married to a man of her own tribe; and she warns you that if you remain longer in the vicinity she cannot prevent her husband and her father from discovering and slaying you."

For a moment Azîz was silent, scarce comprehending the full weight of the blow that had been delivered him. He knew little of man-made marriage bonds—only what he had learned from Nakhla when she told him of the customs of her people. The marriage ceremony her maiden shyness had prevented her from elaborating upon. Only in a general way did Azîz know that certain formalities were observed when a human male took to himself a mate—as to the importance of this custom he had not the slightest conception, as he had no true conception of the significance of any man-made law.

To him there was but one essential to the mating of the sexes—the willingness of both parties. As a child learns, so Azîz had learned largely through the example of others. Aside from Nakhla his sole companions were the savage beasts of the wilderness—when they mated there was no priest—no vows—no ceremonies. Each was content with the other—that alone seemed necessary. Hence his next question.

"And did Nakhla wish to marry this man?" he asked.

"Yes," replied Ben Saada.

Without a word, Azîz turned about and trotted back toward the hills and the beasts. In his throat there was a strange, choking sensation. It was quite new to him, and he was very unhappy. Never had he guessed that such misery existed in all the world as that which he suffered. Physical pain, and he had had his full share of that during the course of his short, brutal life, was as nothing by comparison with this horrible, gnawing, numbing misery for which there could be no healing.

He wanted to be alone. He did not wish to see even his dumb friends; and so he passed north of the canyon where his lair lay and on across the wide strip toward the restless, dismal sea. Only memories of suffering and monotony and hate it aroused within his breast, and so it fitted today so perfectly with his mood that he longed to sit upon its lonely shore mingling his misery with misery of the grey, tumbling waste.

As he walked he removed his burnoose and threw it away. Only Nakhla had bound him to the ways of man. Now that he knew that Nakhla was not for him he was glad to go back to the beasts definitely and forever. The

111

burnoose had always seemed to him rather an aggrava-
tion. It wrapped about his legs when he ran, impeding his
progress. The under garments he had long since dis-
carded, wearing beneath the burnoose only a loin cloth.
This he retained.

Thus unencumbered he moved rapidly toward the sea.
He had just topped the last rise that had hid the broad
Atlantic from him when he saw that which brought him,
beast-like, crouching back in hiding behind a bush. It was
a girl and two men. The former was riding slowly along
the age-old caravan trail that skirts the coast, her mount
stepping daintily, arching his sleek neck and tossing his
head. Azîz could hear the jingle of the curb chain. Behind the girl rode two burnoosed Arabs; but that the girl
was of a different race the youth could see even from a
distance.

Her clothing was light brown and tight fitting. Her head-
dress was unlike anything that he had before seen, and
her skin was white. The little party was moving north
along the trail. They had passed Azîz when the girl
reined in and turning her horse started back toward the
south. Then it was that the youth's indifferent interest in
the three was suddenly transformed to keen excitement.

As the girl approached the two Arabs, whom she had
evidently expected would turn and take their places behind her again, one of them rode close in upon either
side and seizing her bridle reins held her mount. There
ensued a heated discussion. Azîz guessed that the girl first
threatened and then pleaded, though he could not hear
her words; but the men were obdurate, and finally they
turned and rode into the hills a little distance south of
the youth.

Now Azîz' knowledge of matters human was extremely limited. What innate chivalry he possessed required

something more strenuous than had so far occurred to awaken it. He only guessed that the girl accompanied the Arabs against her will, and even had they taken her by an actual demonstration of brute force it might then have been still a question as to what effect the sight of such a thing would have had upon the lad.

The girl was nothing to him. He had never seen either her or the men before. If he had seen two lions attacking a strange lioness would he have felt it incumbent upon himself to rush forward to the she-cat's rescue? However, he determined to follow the three, as here at last seemed a diversion for his distracted mind.

After half an hour he became convinced that the route they were following would lead them straight to the canyon where his den was situated. He smiled as he thought of the reception that would be for them should the lion and his mate be at home—and hungry.

After they had entered the canyon, Azîz was able to approach closer to the trio because of the abundant shelter afforded by the trees and rocks that abounded along the course of the little river. Then it was that he became convinced that the men were taking the girl by force, for twice he saw her attempt to snatch her bridle rein from the hand of him who held it and wheel her horse back down the ravine; but each time the men thwarted her design, scowling fiercely at her and making threatening gestures as they growled in menacing tones at their prisoner.

Near the lion's den were many natural caves upon either side of the ravine. When the three reached this part of the canyon the men drew rein and dismounted. One of them held the horses while the other ascended to a large cave almost directly opposite that which was Azîz' home.

The man entered with his long matchlock at the ready.

After a moment he emerged and called down to his companion. Azîz could hear his words distinctly.

"This will do nicely," he said. "It is close to the river, and there are no indications that el adrea frequents it. Bring the girl."

The other man had by this time dismounted and compelled the girl to do likewise. Now he tethered the horses securely to a large tree; but when he attempted to take the girl upward toward the cave she rebelled, fighting him with all the strength of her frail body.

The youth had crept quite close to these two before the struggle commenced, and now at sight of the helpless girl in the power of the brutal Arab a fierce anger rose within his breast. That the girl was of his own race may have exerted some influence upon his sleeping racial instincts—who may guess?

The first that the two knew that there was another near them was the sound upon their ears of a low, beast-like growl; and then from the brush close at hand leaped an almost naked white man straight for the throat of the Arab. About the stranger's loin cloth was a bandoleer of cartridges, a knife and a pistol; but he seemed to have forgotten these as he went at the son of the desert with naked hands and bared teeth.

The girl looked on in horror at the battle which ensued. The Arab drew his own pistol, but the beast-man wrenched it from his grasp and hurled it to one side, though not before his foeman's fingers had pressed the trigger. Following the report of the firearm there was a sudden movement in a dense thicket upon the hillside opposite the cave to which the Arab had intended dragging his captive, but the actors in the little drama in the canyon's bottom were too engrossed in their own affairs to note what took place above them.

The Arab who had remained with the girl was now down upon his back with Azîz upon him, the teeth of the lion-man buried in his throat. The other Arab was leaping downward to his friend's assistance; and the girl, freed for the moment, had run to her mount to make good the escape which the interference of the stranger had made possible.

She had taken but a half dozen steps toward the tethered animals when a series of frightful roars broke upon her terrified ears, and a glance in the direction of the fearsome sounds revealed two great lions leaping nimbly down the canyonside toward her. They were much too close for her to hope to reach and mount her horse before they should be upon her; and so, with a scream of terror, she turned and raced back toward the battling men.

The roars of the lions and the scream of the girl brought the two Arabs and Azîx from the engrossing occupation of their strife. The youth was not surprised at the presence of the carnivores, and his only fear was for the safety of the girl. The Arabs realizing only the menace to themselves in the charge of the great beasts turned and fled, for Azîz had released his antagonist that he might reach the girl before the lions seized her.

They were almost upon her even now, the huge male in advance of his mate. Azîz leaped toward the frightened creature, roaring out a savage warning to the great beasts behind her. The girl had turned to meet her fate at the same instant, when, to her surprise, both lions turned aside and passed her, so close that the great male brushed her riding breeches.

To her amazement, she saw the huge beast leap to the side of the stranger. She looked to see him rent to shreds; but instead the lions licked his hands; and the lioness, rearing upon her hind feet, placed her forepaws

115

upon his shoulders and rubbed her tawny cheek against his.

The Arabs were by this time making a hasty retreat down the canyon. The youth turned to look for them, and seeing them escaping he waved his hand in their direction, speaking to the two great beasts in a low tone. Like lightning they wheeled, and with mighty bounds, the great muscles rolling beneath their pliant hides and tails straight extended behind them, they raced after the fleeing men.

The girl, her eyes wide in wonderment, watched the death race. There could be but a single outcome, and as the lions came within the last leap of the shrieking men she hid her face in her hands that she might not see the horror of those last moments.

When she looked up once more it was to find the savage white man gazing at her and down the canyon the two lions standing over their kills, looking back toward their master as though awaiting his pleasure. Dumbly she pointed toward them, and Azîz, turning, called softly to his friends.

The girl had meant to point out the menace to themselves of the presence of the two lions. She could not even yet realize that this man was immune from their attack, or that by any possible, human agency could she be protected from them.

At his call they came trotting slowly back, and at the new nearness of them, the girl trembled in terror, stepping involuntarily closer to the half-naked man of whom she would have been almost as terrified as of the lions had she given thought to the matter; but now instinct guided her, and so she turned for protection toward the male of her own species.

"Quick!" she whispered. "Let us escape. They will tear us to pieces."

Azîz turned toward her with a smile.

"Do not fear them," he said. "They are my friends," and then, after a pause—"my only friends."

She clung to his arm in terror as the great beasts approached. They sniffed about her riding boots, and their cold muzzles touched her bare hand where it hung paralyzed at her side.

She saw the man caress them, running his fingers through the great, black mane of the lion and scratching the head of the green-eyed lioness. Even as she saw she could not believe the testimony of her eyes. It was incredible!

She had spoken to him in the tongue of the desert Arabs, for such she supposed him to be, until later she saw that his brown skin was really that of a white man tanned to its present hue by the sun and the winds of the desert and sea.

"Who are you?" asked Azîz.

She told him that she was the daughter of a French colonel whose detachment was stationed at a post a few miles south—a new post that the French government had just established upon the old caravan trail. With great misgivings she asked him if he would accompany her in safety to the camp. To her surprise he assented immediately.

Two of the tethered horses, trembling and terrified in the presence of the lions, had been unable to break their tie-ropes. These the youth brought after sending the lions away, for he saw that it would be impossible for the girl to mount her snorting, plunging beast, or that he could quiet the animal while the great cats were in such close proximity.

At last they succeeded in mounting, after Azîz, knowing that he was going into the presence of white men, had donned one of the Arab's robes. He likewise appropriated one of the long matchlocks which Nakhla had taught him to use. Then he hid the balance of their arms and ammunition in a small cave, against the time that he might find need for them.

Together the two rode down the canyon and across the plain toward the caravan trail—the girl still half afraid of the savage man—the man wondering at the strange beauty of his companion, so different from the beauty of Nakhla.

And thus they came at last to the tents of the French where they were encamped by a river, close to the caravan route, beside which they were to erect a fort, and Azîz saw at close quarters for the first time many men of his own race.

FIFTEEN

Ferdinand and Maria had gone on no honeymoon. Europe was jittery; and no country had extended any invitation, either enthusiastic or otherwise, for the newlyweds to visit it, notwithstanding the fact that several of them had been given ample opportunity—Crown princes and Crown Princesses offered too tempting a target for assassins; so Ferdinand and Maria had had to be content with the hunting lodge, and even that had been very heavily guarded.

Neither of them had had a very pleasant time. Ferdinand was always thinking of Hilda, and Maria was always thinking of her horse face and buckteeth, to say nothing of her bones and her age. Ferdinand didn't help matters any, for he didn't even attempt to be decent to her. He spent his days playing golf or tennis with someone else, and his evenings playing poker with his aides and cronies until long after Maria had gone to sleep.

When they returned to the capital, they went to live at the palace; for Otto could not afford as many palaces as the kings in novels and motion pictures; then they settled down to the humdrum of small-time court life and hating one another.

* * * *

Sarnya and King Otto were discussing problems of State. These related mostly to the purchase of new bombers and other contrivances wherewith to discourage overpopulation of potential enemy countries, and other ways and means of disbursing the generous loan which the unhappy Maria had made possible. While they were talking, Ferdinand came in. They both looked up at him questioningly, their countenances unwreathed in welcoming smiles. Whenever Ferdinand honored them with a visit they were perfectly sure that he was going to ask something of them that they would not want to grant—usually more money.

"Good morning," said Ferdinand.

"Good morning," replied Otto. Sarnya said nothing.

"Isn't it about time that Count Lomsk be permitted to return from exile?" asked Ferdinand. "It seems to me that he has been punished enough. Anyway, he never did anything very bad; and I should like to have him back."

"Why?" asked the King.

"Because he plays a good game of tennis and will help me to forget Maria," explained Ferdinand.

"You are a nasty little cad to speak that way of your wife," said Otto, reprovingly.

"I didn't choose her," Ferdinand reminded; "it was you; and you ought to do something to make it easier for me, if anything ever can."

"Well," said the King, secretly relieved that Ferdinand had not asked for more money, "I see no objection to permitting him to return."

"I do," said Sarnya.

"The others looked at him questioningly. "*You* would," growled Ferdinand.

"What are your reasons, Sarnya?" asked the King.

"He talks to much, he keeps bad company, and he is receiving money from some secret source," explained Sarnya. "We are trying to find out what that source is. We should, therefore, leave him there at least until we have discovered who is financing him and why."

So that was that.

* * * *

One morning Andresy received a message. It was quite short and cryptic. "Tomorrow at midnight," it read; but Andresy read a great deal more in it than those three words, and he immediately got busy.

An hour later William Wesl received a message. It, too, was short; but it was quite understandable to William. It said, "Tonight at the—same place," and it was signed with a dagger that had red ink on the blade. William wondered what the other clerks would think if they knew he had just received a summons from The Terroists. It made him feel very important; but it also nearly scared the pants off him, as the French so quaintly put it. He spent the rest of the day wondering what they wanted of him this time, and was quite certain that at last he was going to be asked to assassinate someone. Now, William didn't want to assassinate anyone. If he could have confined his revolutionary activities to scowling, he would have been perfectly content. The effect upon him of the note was such that the manager had to reprimand him twice and finally threaten him with discharge if he didn't pay more and better attention to his work. But at last the hideous day was over, and William was at home. When he told the cobbler's daughter about the note she nearly had hysterics. She was not a revolutionary and she didn't want William to be. As a matter of fact, William didn't want to be; but, as he explained to the cobbler's daughter, once a revolutionist, always a revolutionist or —a corpse. She said she thought she would go and tell the police; but when she saw how near William came to throwing a fit, she decided that she would not. William finally convinced her that not only his life but hers was at stake—if she reported the matter to the police they would probably shoot him and The Terrorists would kill her. It was the latter argument that prevailed.

When William had been guided to his destination that night, he found himself in the presence of but one man. Andresy showed him a map. It was a map of the palace grounds.

"Now listen very attentively to what I have to say," directed Andresy, "and then repeat it. Fix this map in your mind. Here is a postern gate in the garden wall. You will present yourself there at exactly midnight tomorrow. Be sure to wear gloves. Do not look at the person who admits you. Walk straight ahead to the fountain; then turn squarely to your left and walk toward the palace. When you are about twenty feet from the building, stop. Here is a letter. Put it in your pocket. When a man comes up to you you will be through. You may go out the postern gate and go home."

"Is that all?" asked William.

"That is all," replied Andresy.

"I don't have to shoot anybody."

"No; what put that in your head?"

"I don't know; I—I just thought maybe——"

Andresy laughed. "No, you won't have to shoot anybody; and be very sure that you don't carry any weapon of any kind."

William breathed a sigh of relief. "Of course," he said, "I wouldn't mind killing someone for the cause, only I'm a very poor shot."

"Now go back home," said Andresy, "and keep your mouth shut. Don't tell anyone what you are going to do, especially your wife. Do you understand?"

"Yes, sir," said William.

* * * *

The Italian ambassador waited on the King in the morning. He expressed the felicitations of Il Duce himself, and incidentally of Victor Emmanuel III; then came the ambassador from Germany; and after him, those of France and Great Britain. There was the smell of armaments in the air—armaments and orders. Otto had not felt so important for years. He could almost have kissed Maria —almost, but not quite. He sent for the Officer of the Guard. When he came, the King looked surprised. He did not recognize the man, and he thought that he knew every officer of The Guards.

"Who are you?" he demanded.

"I am Captain Carlyn, sir, Officer of the Guard. I was told to report to you."

"Oh, yes," said Otto; "I seem to recall the name. Let's see; you're a friend of the Crown Prince, are you not?"

"His Royal Highness has been so gracious as to befriend me, sir," replied Carlyn.

"Yes, yes," said Otto. "I wish to inspect the 10th Regiment of Cavalry today. You will make the necessary arrangements. I shall be there at three o'clock this afternoon."

* * * *

"I have to go out tonight," said William, after dinner, "but you must not ask me where I am going. It is very important business for the cause. I am becoming a most important person in the inner circles. After the revolution, there is no telling what I may be—a cabinet minister, perhaps. We shall have a car of our own, then; and maybe we shall live in a palace. When the people get what belongs to them, we shall all live in palaces."

"There are not enough palaces," said the cobbler's daughter, "and anyway I should not care to take care of a palace. I have enough work to do taking care of three rooms now."

"Don't be silly," said William. "You will have many servants."

"How can I have servants if everyone is going to live in a palace? Do you suppose people would leave their palaces to come and work for us?"

William scratched his head. "That is the trouble with you women," he said; "you never understand anything. These are matters for men."

* * * *

It was just midnight as William approached the postern gate. He was quite nervous, but he did just as he had been instructed to do. When the gate opened, he walked in without looking to right or left and went straight to the fountain; then he turned to the left and walked to within about twenty feet of the palace. Most of the windows in that wing of the palace were dark, and there were only a few dim lights in the grounds outside. It was quite dark where William stood because the King's bedchamber was on that side of the palace, on the second floor, just above William; and the King did not like to have lights shining into his room.

William put his hand in his pocket to make sure that he still had the letter he was supposed to deliver to some mysterious person. He crumpled it a little in searching for it, because of the gloves he wore. He wondered why it had been necessary for him to wear gloves. Those Terrorists were certainly peculiar people. Everything they did seemed most unusual to William, but then it was just as well to do what they said to do and ask no questions. He thought he had gotten off very well indeed in having been asked merely to deliver a letter instead of having to assassinate someone and get himself shot or hanged. He felt quite important, but he also felt a little nervous. Suppose someone should come and ask him what he was doing in the palace gardens. Andresy had told him what to say in such an eventuality, but William could visualize far-reaching repercussions of such a reply. He had been told to say that he had an assignation with a scullery maid who was employed in the palace. He was even given the maid's name. That would be a very difficult thing to explain to the cobbler's pretty daughter. William heard the clock strike half past twelve then one. He wished that the mysterious stranger would come and get his letter. William was getting sleepy.

As the clock struck half past one, William heard two shots. They came from the interior of the palace, directly above him; then something struck the ground close to him. He did not see what it was.

SIXTEEN

For six weeks the youth remained the guest of Colonel Joseph Vivier whose daughter, Marie, he had rescued from the two Arab servants who had attempted to abduct her.

The French officer took a deep interest in the strange story of the young man's life; but question him as he would he could not get back of the time that Azîz had come to the deck of the strange steamer.

Much of his story seemed too weird and unreal for credence, so that at last the Frenchman came to doubt it all, although he took a liking to the narrator and did what he could to make his stay at the camp pleasant.

Marie also took a lively interest in the stranger, and when she discovered that his only language was broken and imperfect Arabic she set to work to teach him French, as well to read and write as to speak it.

But all this time Azîz was very unhappy. His mind dwelt much upon Nakhla and her cruelty to him. It seemed impossible that she should have chosen another mate, for although no actual words of love had passed between them he realized now that he had considered her his, though he had not sufficient knowledge then of the ways of men to know how to make a declaration of his affection.

Yet had not the stranger told him that Nakhla was married to another? In his unsophistication he had not yet come to realize that most men consider the gift of speech solely as a means of defeating the purposes of truth. He believed the stranger, he who had never yet himself deceived.

Colonel Vivier clothed Azîz in khaki riding clothes, and set him to attending Marie when she rode abroad, as she did daily, into the hills or the desert. In a way he was half servant and half companion. He ate at the same table with the colonel and his daughter, yet their attitude toward him was one of charitable condescension, for was not Vivier a direct descendant of that famous Count de Vivier of the reign of Louis XIV? And this nameless stranger? Who indeed was he?

One day Colonel Vivier set forth with a small escort to ride upon a friendly visit to a neighboring sheik. Marie begged to be allowed to accompany him, and as she usually had her own way the matter was quickly settled to her satisfaction—she and Azîz might come.

The lion-man paid little attention to the direction of their march—he was engrossed in conversation with the vivacious French girl. They had become the best of friends—even the colonel, ordinarily most unobserving, had recently become a little concerned at the growing intimacy of the two.

It was not until the little column had halted before the douar of a native sheik that Azîz realized the identity of their destination—it was the camp of Sheik Ali-Es-Hadji! The lion-man's heart came suddenly to his throat as the familiar surroundings recalled the happiness that he had lost; but no word escaped him.

With the others he rode close to the desert people, who, half suspicious, had come forward to inspect the visitors. He was sitting on his horse close beside Marie Vivier when his attention was suddenly attracted to the doorway of a nearby tent. Framed in the entrance stood

Nakhla, her wide eyes fastened upon his face, one hand upon her rapidly rising and falling bosom.

"What a beautiful girl," whispered Miss Vivier to her companion.

At the sound of her voice the eyes of the Arab girl turned toward her. Then Azîz called a friendly greeting to her. Again her eyes returned to him, but now they were blazing. She tossed her little chin in the air, and without so much as an acknowledgment of his salutation, turned her back full upon him and went back into the tent.

"Evidently she does not approve of strangers," said Marie.

Azîz did not answer. In the goat-skin tent before them, unseen, there lay stretched upon a great rug from Persia an unhappy girl, her stifled breathing broken by pitiful sobs.

There was another in the camp of Sheik Ali-Es-Hadji who had recognized Azîz, and when the French rode away after the termination of their friendly visit he went to the tent where Nakhla was, and entering found her still weeping there upon the great rug of many colors.

He called her name, but she did not look up—only motioned him away. Still the man stood—a grim smile of satisfaction upon his cruel lips.

"Come, Nakhla," he said after a long silence. "Let us be friends. It is not my fault that the white man cleaves to the white woman. It is as it should be, and thee and me, who are children of the desert, should not look beyond the desert's rim for our mates. Let the white man have his white woman—already, I am told, they are married after the manner of the French—and let me have thee."

Nakhla sprang to her feet, her eyes blazing.

"I would not have you, Ben Saada," she cried, "were there no other man upon earth. What care I for the white man? You are a fool, Ben Saada. It is nothing to me that the white man has married. I hate him. Go away and do not annoy me; but remember this—I shall not marry you or any other man. All men are fools and liars."

Ben Saada had hoped that the sight of the stranger with a white girl would prove a strong argument in favor of his suit. He had lied to Azîz to get rid of him, and now fate had played directly into his hands to convince Nakhla that the white man loved another; so now that he saw that the girl was no more reconciled to him than before it threw him into a rage. He went out of the tent scowling darkly and muttering incoherently to himself.

The sheik was approaching the tent as Ben Saada emerged. The latter stopped him.

"Ali-Es-Hadji," he said, "the time has come when I must have Nakhla. She is still rebellious. Is it right that the daughter should rule the sire? You are master, Ali-Es-Hadji, and twenty camels is the return I would give to have Nakhla for my wife."

"She will not have you, Ben Saada," replied the old sheik.

"She will have me," answered Ben Saada, "or a white man will take her as his plaything. Are you blind, Ali-Es-Hadji, that you did not see with eyes she looked upon the white man who rode beside the Frenchman's daughter today? I found her weeping in your tent because of jealousy. And do you think that the white man will not take advantage of her mad love at the first opportunity? It was to see her that they came today. Unless you give me your daughter in marriage, they will come back and steal her away; unless it happens that she goes of her own volition to the arms of the white man. And do you know, Ali-Es-Hadji, who this white stranger is? No, even you do not guess. I, who have seen Nakhla meet him in the desert, know the truth. He is the naked beast-man who came with el adrea to rob your flocks. I know, for I saw Nakhla with him one night within the corral."

At that instant both men turned to see Nakhla standing in the doorway of the tent looking at them. There was an expression of contempt upon her face as she looked at Ben Saada. Ali-Es-Hadji, her father, turned toward her.

"You have heard?" he asked.

"I have heard," she answered.

"Does Ben Saada speak the truth?" asked the sheik.

"What he says about my meeting the lion-man is the truth," replied Nakhla; "but that they will come and steal me, or that I will go to the white man is a lie, and you, Ali-Es-Hadji, my father, know that it is a lie. Ben Saada is a dog. He wishes to marry me that some day he may be sheik. I shall not mate with him—first will I kill myself."

"You shall marry only whom you please, my daughter," said Ali-Es-Hadji. "I have spoken; and you, Ben Saada, have heard. Let this end the matter," and he turned and entered his tent with Nakhla.

Ben Saada was furious. Plans for revenge surged through his brain, and at last a great and wicked determination found lodgement there. He went to a half dozen of his cronies—wicked, vicious fellows of the younger warriors. They mounted their fleet horses and rode out into the desert that they might talk without danger of being overheard.

Late that night they returned, and while three crept within the corral with the animals the balance held the horses close without. Presently one who had gone within returned with a saddled horse, and turning it over to one of those who had remained outside he returned. Then upon the night air their rose, low and ominous, the growl of a lion. It came from the corral.

Nakhla heard it. Her heart stopped beating. Trembling she came to her feet and crept to the door of her tent. The camp was asleep. There was no moon. In the darkness she crept toward the corral, but only after a bitter storm of contending emotions had raged within her. Her first impulse had been to hasten out in answer to the call, and then had come a sudden burst of mad jealousy that had held her back.

Before her memory rose vividly the picture of the fair skinned girl and the man in khaki whom she had seen laughing and talking with her—as easily and familiarly as ever he had talked with Nakhla. And the clothes! The white man's garmenture seemed to Nakhla to have brought a strange metamorphosis in the lion-man—they had transferred him to another sphere, a sphere beyond her reach, to which she might not possibly hope to attain.

But notwithstanding her jealousy and her hopelessness, love conquered in the end, drawing her to the corral, from which again had arisen the low lion-like growl in which however was the palpable note of imitation which led her to assume that it was Azîz calling her.

Scarce had she entered the enclosure than a man seized her from either side, quickly binding a scarf about her mouth that she might not scream aloud. She struggled, but her resistance was futile. Her captors half carried half dragged her to the opposite side of the corral, lifted her over the wall, and a moment later swung her to the back of her own El Djebel.

Still in silence they leaped to the backs of their own

horses. There was the soft sound of galloping hoofs upon sand, and the little party had vanished into the desert darkness beneath the moonless sky.

It was a sad and silent Azîz who rode back to the camp of the French at the side of Marie Vivier. The girl, ignorant of the cause of his preoccupation, rattled on gaily, first upon one subject, then another until finally she hit upon the one subject of all others that was closest to the man's heart and yet the one which, of all others, he would rather not have spoken.

"I cannot," said Marie, "forget the beautiful face of the girl in the tent door, or the strange, half frightened expression with which she discovered us. I imagine that it was the natural fear and timidity of the half wild desert born strangers of another race."

Azîz did not reply. They were almost to the encampment now—in a few minutes he would be free to go to his own tent and grieve in solitude after the manner of the beasts from which he had derived the ethics of his existence.

As they rode into the cantonment of the troops two strange officers and two white women rose from before the colonel's tent, the men saluting and the women waving a smiling greeting to the commandant.

Colonel Vivier turned his command over to his major and trotted forward to greet the newcomers—they were two of the officers and their wives who had been on leave when the regiment left Algiers and had just rejoined after a visit in Paris.

It was Azîz' custom to accompany Marie to her father's tent, where, after she had dismounted, he took her horse and led it to the picket line, turning it over there to a trooper. Now as he dismounted and assisted the girl to the ground he saw the eyes of the strangers upon him, and Marie seeing their questioning looks hastened to introduce him.

As soon as possible he withdrew with the horses; and after he had gone many were the questions that were asked about him, for his remarkable physique, which not even the clothing of civilization could entirely hide, and his handsome face had awakened the curiosity of the two women.

One of them, a Madam Semeler, seemed rather shocked at the idea of the apparent familiarity between the stranger and the colonel's daughter; and as she was the wife of Vivier's senior captain and a woman who had taken it upon herself to assume toward Marie the responsibilities of her dead mother, she lost no time in making it quite plain that she disapproved of the friendly relations that had sprung up between the friendless outcast and the colonel's family.

She did not say much before Marie, but at the first opportunity she drew Vivier to one side and poured her fears into his ear. At first the colonel laughed at her; but finally, backed by information that she had evidently gained from officers who had been in camp when they arrived and before the colonel and his detachment had returned from his visit to Sheik Ali-Es-Hadji, she succeeded in arousing the good man's doubts, at least as to the propriety of his daughter's continued unchaperoned association with the lion-man.

Azîz and Marie, ignorant of the gossip the meddling woman had initiated, had strolled down to the beach after the evening meal, where they stood watching the surf and admiring the graceful play of the propoises as they rose slowly and majestically above the surface.

For some time neither had spoken, when, quite irrelevantly, Marie returned to the subject which their return to camp earlier in the day had interrupted.

"I was just thinking," she said, "how strange it is that so beautiful a girl as the one we saw at Ali-Es-Hadji's this morning should not be married—these Arab girls are usually betrothed at a very early age, and one of her beauty cannot fail having many admirers."

"How do you know she is not married?" asked Azîz.

"Her eyebrows are not connected," replied Marie, "and among all the tribes with whose customs I am familiar the connecting of the eyebrows by a straight line is a certain indication of wifehood."

Azîz thought for a long time after this. He was trying to reconcile this information with the word that the Arab horseman had brought to him out upon the desert that day that his life had been turned from a song into a dirge.

Marie, too, was musing. She had accidentally overheard some of Madam Semeler's conversation with the wife of another officer, and with sudden awakened loyalty toward Azîz she had determined to discover all that she might which could prove that he was the gentleman she, in her generous heart, felt him to be. If she could but find some clue to his identity! She did not for a moment mistrust him or the strange story that he had told, though her father had always been rather skeptical, attributing the tale to some mental defect superinduced by the dangers and suffering to which the youth must have been exposed during his lonely life among the beasts.

"Azîz," she said at last, "have you no recollection of any other name than that which you now bear?"

"None," he replied.

"Who gave you that name?" she continued. "It must have been your mother, for none but a mother would have bestowed it upon you—unless," and she smiled, "you have had a sweetheart. And if your mother gave it to you you must remember her or you would not remember the name. Tell me, can't you recall your mother or your father?"

"Why could my name have been given me only by my mother—or my sweetheart?" asked the lion-man, and his heart beat strong within his breast as he awaited her reply.

"Can it be that you don't know its meaning?" asked Marie.

"I don't know," he replied, "that it means any more than any other name—it merely is useful to distinguish me from others. Has it any special meaning, then?"

Marie laughed. "And you really don't know the meaning of Azîz?" she asked.

"No, I don't," replied the youth. "Tell me—what does it signify?"

"In Arabic, Azîz," explained Marie, "your name means 'beloved'."

SEVENTEEN

The night that William Wesl waited in the palace gardens to deliver a letter to a mysterious stranger, Prince Ferdinand spent at the hunting lodge playing contract with several officers of the Guard, among whom were two who had never been invited to one of the Prince's private gatherings before. These two were proteges of General Count Sarnya, and quite generally suspected in court circles of being members of his feared secret police.

Ferdinand was nervous and irritable all during the evening, jumping at the slightest sound. He played atrociously, which was unusual for Ferdinand, paying no attention to discards and bidding recklessly on four card suits after denial by his partner. He lost heavily and drank even more heavily. When the telephone rang between one-thirty and two, while he was making for the next hand, he turned very white and dropped the deck to the floor.

* * * *

King Otto retired at a quarter before one; by one o'clock he was asleep. At twenty-nine minutes after one a man entered his room. He stood listening for thirty seconds; then he approached the bed where the King lay, passing around the foot of the bed and standing beside it between the bed and the window. The man made scarcely any noise; but the King, who was a light sleeper, awakened. He opened his eyes to see a man standing over him. In the dim light, he could see that the man was in uniform and wore white gloves. The King sat up.

"Who are you?" he demanded.

For answer, the man shot him twice through the heart; then he tossed the pistol out of the window, and ran from the room through the King's study.

Captain Carlyn, Officer of the Guard, was the first man into the King's bedroom after the shots were fired. He saw the King lying with his head over the side of the bed, but he paid no attention to the King. Instead he ran directly to the open window, drawing his service pistol. Below him, between the palace and the fountain, he saw a shadowy figure. Captain Carlyn, asking no question, giving no warning, immediately opened fire. William Wesl, surprised, terrified, hesitated a moment; then turned and fled. The Officer of the Guard emptied his pistol at the fleeing figure. The last shot struck William in the left shoulder, the bullet penetrating his heart. Armed men, pouring into the gardens from the palace and gate found a little figure slumped in death beside the fountain. They also found a pistol lying beneath the bedroom window of the murdered king, and when they searched William's body, they found a sealed note, typewritten, which read, "I did this because I hate kings. I had no confederates nor accomplices."

"He was very clever," said one of the officers who investigated the assassination. "There were no fingerprints on the pistol, because he wore gloves. If he had escaped by the postern gate, he might never have been apprehended. It was only Captain Carlyn's quick wit and marksmanship that avenged the King."

The pistol they found was a .32 caliber automatic. The empty shells on the floor of the King's bedroom and the bullets in his heart were also .32 caliber. The service pistol of the Officer of the Guard was a .45 caliber. It was a .45 caliber bullet that had killed William Wesl. All these things came out at the inquest; but when they traced the pistol by its serial number, police records showed that it had been purchased by a Lieutenant Hans de Groot of the 10th Regiment of Cavalry, which looked pretty bad for Hans for a short time, until his testimony that the pistol had been stolen from his quarters several weeks before was substantiated by the testimony of Captain Carlyn, who stated that he was a close frined of Lieutenant de Groot and distinctly recalled that the latter had told him at the time of the theft of his pistol.

The authorities were delighted that the affair had been cleared up so easily, and relieved to know that it had been the work of a weak-minded individual and not the outcome of a Terrorist plot; so everyone was happy except the cobbler's pretty daughter.

The question as to how the assassin gained entrance to the palace and penetrated to the King's bedroom without being seen, remained an unsolved mystery, as did the fact that he had jumped from a second-story window onto turf without leaving any imprint on the ground; but of course Captain Carlyn, who, as Officer of the Guard, made the initial investigation did the best that he could under the circumstances; and that is all that should be expected of anyone.

* * * *

When the telephone rang at the hunting lodge between one-thirty and two that morning, and the Crown Prince dropped the cards on the floor, an aide picked up the telephone receiver and took the message. He was very white as he hung up and turned toward the little company of men; then he stood up very straight and clicked his heels together.

"The King is dead," he said. "Long live the King!"

Otto was given a most impressive funeral. Two kings walked behind the flag-draped gun carriage that bore the body of the dead monarch—his son and the father of Queen Maria—and there were many princes and dignitaries of the state and church and a great cortege of armed troops. The streets were lined with lesser people, some of whom sat on the curbs and ate their lunches from paper bags. There was a holiday air that belied the bier on the gun carriage and the lugubrious music of the military bands. The people had come to look and enjoy, not to mourn. They might have been congregating for an Iowa picnic in Sycamore Grove, but for time and place.

As it must to all men, death had come to Otto; and nobody gave a damn.

EIGHTEEN

Two things Azîz had learned within the course of a very few minutes—two things that might mean to him all the difference in the world between misery and happiness. He could scarcely wait to learn the truth. It seemed that Marie would never be done looking at the silly sea—the happy, laughing, dancing sea. A moment before it had been a sad and weeping sea.

But at last the French girl turned back toward the father's tent. The newcomers were within; so the lion-man begged off when Marie urged him to join them, and bidding the girl good-night hastened to his own tent.

His plans were made. He would ride that night, fast and furious, to the douar of Sheik Ali-Es-Hadji. He would know the truth. Evidently there had been a great mistake—the lone horseman had brought him a lie instead of the truth.

He had buckled on his revolver, and seized his rifle, and was on the point of hurrying down to the picket line to saddle his horse, when it suddenly occurred to him that the horse, the accouterments, the clothes that he wore even, were his only through the courtesy of Colonel Vivier—it would never do to ride away at night without making some sort of explanation to his host and patron.

So instead of going to the picket line he hastened off in the direction of Vivier's tent, but he never entered it, for at the threshold he heard his own name upon the lips of one within. Such knowledge of the niceties of civilized conduct as one might derive from a lifetime of association with a black-maned lion was Azîz's. To this, of

course, there had been added that which he had been
able to absorb from Nakhla and Marie, but at that he
did not possess sufficient to deter him from untroubled
listening to that which went on beyond the frail canvas
wall.

"What do you know of this Azîz person, anyway,
Marie?" a woman's voice was saying. "For aught you or
the colonel know he is an escaped convict, hiding in the
desert. A forger, maybe, or a murderer, even."

"Poof! Helen," came the colonel's voice. "Look at the
man's eyes—they're honest to the bottom of them—and
clean. I tell you Azîz is all right."

"That he is," exclaimed Marie.

"Well," continued the woman's voice, in that exas-
perating air of superior finality that brooks no contrary
opinion, "well, she is your daughter, of course. Colonel
Vivier; but I loved her poor mother, and I feel that it is
my duty to do my poor best to preserve Marie from such
a misalliance."

"Misalliance!" gasped Colonel Vivier, coming half to
his feet. "Misalliance? Mon Dieu! Do you think that Marie
intends wedding this fellow!" and he glanced quickly toward his daughter.

Azîz could hear through the canvas wall but through it
he could not see what Colonel Vivier saw—a sudden
scarlet flush suffuse the face of the French girl.

"It has reached a point," broke in the woman's voice,
"where the whole regiment is talking about it—and talking about little else."

"Madam Semeler!" cried Marie, reproachfully, but she
got no further.

"Misalliance!" almost shouted Colonel Vivier. "How
dare any member of my regiment link the name of their
colonel's daughter with that of an outcast—a waif—an

unknown, nameless fellow who is but a grade above a servant in my household! It is outrageous. Do you think for a moment that the daughter of the house of Vivier—a descendant of the famous Count de Vivier—could so degrade herself as to entertain such an idea! We have befriended the poor devil—that is all. We know nothing about him, except that he does not presume upon our friendship," and he looked meaningly at Madam Semeler. "Has he ever presumed, Marie," he asked, turning toward his daughter, "to assume toward you anything more than the quasi-menial position he holds?"

Azîz did not linger to hear more. He had heard quite enough. There was no rancor in his heart toward Vivier. Something told him that the man had spoken honestly and that he still was what Azîz had always thought him— his best friend; but the lion-man's eyes had been opened to a new thread in the intricate human fabric called civilized society, to an understanding of his place in that society.

Evidently, regardless of character and deportment, all men were not equal. There seemed to be an indefinable something which made Colonel Vivier one sort of person and Azîz another. Azîz was of a lower order—he was of the "servant" class—he could never hope to associate upon a plane of perfect equality with these superior beings. Of course, he did not understand it at all—all that he knew was something rose up within him in rebellion— but greater even than this was a feeling of bitter humiliation and a poignant hurt that depressed him.

If he was not good enough for Marie Vivier, then most certainly he could never hope to aspire to so radiant a thing as Nakhla. He was moving back toward his tent as these dismal thoughts passed through his mind. Slowly he entered his little canvas home. Slowly and deliberately he removed every article of clothing and equipment that had been furnished him by Colonel Vivier.

At last he stood naked except for his loin cloth and bandoleer. In his belt were the knife and revolver he had taken from the marauder chieftain. In his right hand the rifle that had belonged to the traitorous servant of Marie. He would go away, nor would he take aught that might obligate him in any way to these superior people who considered him so far beneath them.

The sentries knew him for a favored friend of their colonel; so he might easily have passed them clothed in khaki, but whether or not they would permit him to go forth in his nakedness he did not know, for their suspicions might be aroused, in which event they would report the matter to their commandant before they allowed him to pass.

Azîz did not care to be subjected to anything of the sort. He was free. No one could detain him. He could come and go as he saw fit. And so it was that a wild beast, silent and stealthy as the lion that had trained him, passed out of the camp of the French soldiers so close to a sentry that the fellow might have touched it with his bayonet had he known of its presence.

Straight back toward his savage lair he trotted through the dark and moonless night; but as he went, he thought; and the more he thought the more impossible it seemed to him that he could live without Nakhla. Human companionship had grown to mean a great deal more to him than he could possibly imagine, and the personification of humanity was to him the wondrous daughter of Sheik Ali-Es-Hadji. Nor had the lion-man's perspicacity been one whit at fault in its estimate of the bronze maid of the desert. Far above the average of her sisters, was Nakhla—not only in personal beauty, but in virtue, goodness, character and intelligence as well. A girl in a thousand, was she—yes, in ten thousand, in whom race or complexion might bear no slightest place in the estimate that was her due. Nakhla of the Sahara was a daughter of the races.

And something of all this found lodgment that night in the mind of Azîz, so that the lure of this perfect maid carried him past the lair of his savage mates—on and upward through the Stygian blackness of the canyon toward the pass that leads eastward out into the Sahara.

Thoughtless of self, the man forged ahead. The two great bodies lying in the brush close beside the watering place above the den went all unnoticed. The savage, flaming eyes caught no answering spark from the introspective orbs of the lion-man. Azîz was too deeply engrossed in what was transpiring within his own handsome head to note the sudden movement of two soft-footed creatures close behind him as he passed through the ford to the opposite side of the river where the travelling was better.

But he was suddenly brought to consciousness of things less remote by the hurtling of two giant bodies against him, bodies that hurled him forward upon his face beneath their great weight. However far his thoughts may have been wandering they returned with lightning-like rapidity to the comprehension that two lions were upon him.

If they were not his lions here was an end of him and all his troubles; and if they were his lions he could not but recall that it had been some time since they had seen him; and the chance obtruded itself upon his consciousness that even though they proved to be his lions they might not remember him, for he had learned of late that the

142

minds and memories of beasts may not be gauged by human standards.

But even in the instant that these thoughts passed through his mind, and while he struggled beneath the giant bodies above him, he heard the purring of one of the beasts in his ear and then felt the rough tongue upon his cheek.

With a laugh of relief he put his arms about the neck of the lion and drawing the great head close down to his pressed his face against the savage, wrinkled jowl of his first friend.

So great was the joy of the beasts in seeing him again that it was some time before he could gain his feet, as they kept pouncing upon him with the playfulness of kittens; but at least he stood erect, an arm about the neck of each of the huge cats.

For a while he remained there, stroking and caressing them; but his mind was settled upon his immediate future, and so with a final hug for each he left them, trotting on across the hills and out into the desert.

It was dawn when he came to the douar of Sheik Ali-Es-Hadji. Already the breakfast fires were burning, and burnoosed Arabs were moving hither and thither about the encampment. Unhesitatingly Azîz approached the tents. At sight of him several of the warriors ran forward, their weapons ready; but as he called to them in their own tongue, asking for Nakhla, they drew about him curiously, for never had they seen so strange a figure as this almost naked white giant.

The commotion brought Ali-Es-Hadji from his tent, and when he learned that the stranger had come in search of his daughter he strode forward to interview him, his face stern and forbidding.

At sight of him he knew that it was the lion-man, and on the instant, recalling Ben Saada's prophesies, he became suspicious. His keen glance took in the youth from head to foot. He noted the superb physique, the strong cut face, the clear eyes, the dignity of the man's carriage. Despite himself Ali-Es-Hadji was impressed.

"Who are you?" he asked, "and what brings you to my tent?"

"I am—" the youth hesitated to give the name that Nakhla had called him—"I am the brother of el adrea; and I have come to have speech with Nakhla, the daughter of Sheik Ali-Es-Hadji."

"What would you of the daughter of Ali-Es-Hadji?" asked the sheik. "I am he—what would you of my daughter?"

"I would learn if she be married to another," replied Azîz, "for I would have her for myself."

Ali-Es-Hadji's face went black with anger.

"You!" he cried. "You, dog of a Nasrâny—naked white beggar—you have the temerity to aspire to the daughter of a great sheik? You—a worthless vagabond without a following—without even a burnoose to your back. Where, pig, would you find the twenty camels with which to pay me for my daughter's hand, even if she would have such vermin as you?"

Azîz' level gaze never left the face of the old Arab. If his heart was torn with misery and his breast with indignation and with rage, his face showed naught of the emotions which rioted beneath his smooth bronzed hide. Last night he had learned in what low esteem the men of his own race held him. Now he had discovered that the wild desert Arab looked down upon him as an inferior being. Indeed was he an outcast and a pariah. Did Nakhla also consider him as dirt beneath her feet? Was he to her also but as camel dung?

"Let me speak with Nakhla," he persisted. "If Nakhla says that I am a pig and a dog I will go away."

Ali-Es-Hadji was about to refuse the request, and Azîz seeing his decision in the expression of his face sought to forestall it.

"Since Nakhla told me that it was wrong," he said, "to tamper with her father's flocks, neither I nor my lions have come down to the douar of Ali-Es-Hadji; but if I go away, leaving my lions here, who will there be to prevent them coming nightly to your corral? Or if you refuse my request why should I not then be your enemy, bringing my two great beasts often among your herds and your people? Even now the lioness is big with cubs, and in a year there may be four or five lions where now there are but three. Would you be happy in the knowledge that five lions were constantly seeking to slay you and your people and your cattle? Would it not be better to be friends with the brother of el adrea? Even though Nakhla tells me that she no longer likes me, I will be no enemy to her people; but if you refuse to let me speak with her I shall know that you are my enemy indeed."

Now Ali-Es-Hadji, though a brave man, contemplated with horror the suggestion that five lions might be brought to prey upon him. He had it in his mind that the young man might be easily killed before he could leave the douar, but that would not preserve him from the depredations of the lions. His only hope lay in placating the lion-man, and with this thought in view he determined to see Nakhla first and require her to send her savage friend away in peace, but permanently.

"Wait here," he said to Azîz. "I will fetch my daughter."

Then he entered the tent that was reserved for Nakhla in the rear of his own. A moment later he reappeared— an expression of apprehension on his face. He turned to several of the women who stood upon the edge of the curious crowd that was eyeing the lion-man.

"Where is Nakhla?" he asked. "Who has seen my daughter this morning?"

The women looked from one to another, each signifying her ignorance of the whereabouts of the chief's daughter by a shake of the head. Ali-Es-Hadji commanded several of the younger women to search for her. Presently they returned to say that Nakhla was not within the douar and that El Djebel, her horse, was gone likewise.

At this moment the figure of a horseman could be seen galloping swiftly toward the douar from across the desert. Streaming in the wind behind him waved the graceful folds of his burnoose above the rising and falling back of his white mount. The two seemed alive with tidings— the gait of the horse, the attitude of the man proclaimed that they were bearers of important information, perhaps, they thought, concerning Nakhla.

Ali-Es-Hadji and his people stood silently awaiting their coming, as though something told them that the two brought word from the missing Nakhla. Beside Ali-Es-Hadji stood Azîz, the lion-man, awaiting in silence the coming of the messenger.

There was a rush of feet as the Arab galloped at full speed among the tents and in a final cloud of flying sand and dust threw his horse to its haunches at the very feet of the sheik.

It was Brebisch, friend and confederate of Ben Saada. He did not dismount. His attitude was of one who in his own heart doubts the welcome that awaits him. Beneath his burnoose one hand grasped his long pistol. Brebisch was prepared for any eventuality.

"Ali-Es-Hadji," he cried, and his tone was almost defiant, "I bring you the greetings of Ben Saada and word that your daughter is well in his keeping. Ben Saada will wed her if you send him assurance of your friendship, and he will return and live beneath your tent; but if you will not promise Ben Saada your protection then he bids me tell you that he will keep your daughter anyway—but that he will not wed her."

Brebisch was silent, evidently awaiting Ali-Es-Hadji's reply. The face of the sheik was a study in fear and rage and sorrow well controlled. Only his long, strong fingers opened and closed convulsively as though already they could feel the throat of the seducer of his daughter in their grip. His old eyes blazed with the fire of his unconquered forebears as he replied to the messenger from Ben Saada.

"Tell Ben Saada," he said slowly, "that Ali-Es-Hadji does not treat with renegades and traitors. I shall come and get him, and if he has harmed my daughter he shall die, staked out upon the desert to fill the bellies of the jackal and the vulture with his putrid meat. That is the only answer that Ali-Es-Hadji has to send to Ben Saada. Begone!"

Brebisch made no reply, but wheeling his horse galloped out into the desert in the direction from which he had come. For a long time old Ali-Es-Hadji remained in thought, his eyes bent upon the ground. Then he turned toward Azîz, but Azîz was not there. Instead, far out upon the desert, a savage beast trotted doggedly along the spoor of a flying horseman.

NINETEEN

A few days after Otto had been laid to rest and the first untroubled sleep he had enjoyed since his accession, a delegation waited upon King Ferdinand with a draft of the new constitution. He refused to grant them an audience. General Count Sarnya advised him to reconsider.

"I am king," stated Ferdinand, arrogantly, "and I shall remain king. I shall not resign my power to *hoi polloi.*"

"Remember your father, your cousin, and your uncle," Sarnya reminded him; "they seemed to have incurred the displeasure of *hoi polloi.*"

"We are not afraid," replied Ferdinand pompously.

"You are a fool, Ferdinand," said Sarnya. "I should like to help you, but I can tell you now that your only hope is to make peace with the revolutionary party. It is headed by a man named Andresy. He is earnest and a real patriot. His followers will do anything that he tells them to. I think they are all fools, but to us they are as a thousand to one. I have tried to combat them for years, but they only grow in strength. Your father antagonzied them. If you are conciliatory, you may remain king for years. You will not rule, but you will live."

The next day, General Count Sarnya received an order relieving him of his duties as Chief of Staff and appointing him to command of the frontier forces. The same day, Count Maximilian Lomsk returned from exile, bringing the little blonde from Germany with him.

* * * *

"Your Majesty," said Captain Carlyn, "Count Lomsk is boasting that he is to be Chief of Staff. I had hoped that your Majesty would honor me with that appointment."

Ferdinand fidgeted. He was very much afraid of the sinister Carlyn. "We have not reached a decision in that matter," he said; and the next day Captain Carlyn was transferred to a regiment on the frontier. That was his answer.

* * * *

Hilda de Groot clung to Ferdinand. "I thought you would never come," she whispered. "I thought that now that you were king, I should never see you again."

"You are going to see more of me than ever," he said. "I am going to build a palace just for you and me. In the meantime you are coming to the royal palace as lady-in-waiting to Maria."

Hilda shuddered. "I couldn't do that," she cried. "What would Maria think?"

"It makes no difference what she thinks. I am king."

* * * *

"It has been a long time since I have seen you, my friend," said Andresy.

"You know how careful I have had to be," replied Carlyn.

"And now?" asked Andresy.

"The fool has transferred me to the frontier, and is going to appoint Count Max Lomsk Chief of Staff and head of the secret police."

"What is to be done about it? Of course, the idiot is digging his own grave. The question is, how best to get him into it quickly. Since he refused to see the delegation that waited on him with the new constitution, I have feared the worst. We shall have to do something. Have you any suggestions?"

"Yes. There is a young lieutenant in the 10th Cavalry whom you should know. He is all right. I have been working on him for a long time."

"Who is he?"

"Hans de Groot, the brother of Hilda de Groot."

Andresy whistled. "Oh," he said, "I think I see. He does not like Ferdinand."

"He does not," replied Carlyn.

"Arrange a meeting," directed Andresy.

* * * *

Ferdinand paced up and down the room. Maria was in tears. "Do you think," she demanded, "that I will remain for one minute under the same roof with that woman?"

"Do as you please," said Ferdinand. "Whether you like it or not, she is coming."

"I shall go home," announced Maria.

"That will only make a scandal," said Ferdinand; "and if you do go home, I shall divorce you for desertion."

"I shall see to it that you never get a divorce; and, furthermore, I shall tell my father to call your loans."

* * * *

Hilda had two new motors and many magnificent jewels. She also had her choice of the crown jewels, but she was not happy in the palace. She was amazed at the variety and number of ways people could invent to snub her subtly. Unfortunately, perhaps, for her, she was neither ambitious nor vengeful; had she been, she could have made things most uncomfortable for those who snubbed her. Hilda's first mistake had lain in loving a crown prince. It was greatly magnified now that he was king. Gardener's daughters should not do such things.

Maria had gone back to papa; and while nobody at Ferdinand's court had liked her while she was there, they all appeared desolated now that she had left. Overnight, she seemed to have acquired more fine and lovable characteristics than even a doting mother might discern in an angel child.

No, Hilda was not happy; neither was Ferdinand. He had received a reminder through the ambassador from the court of his father-in-law that the first interest payment on the nuptial loan was overdue, and that if it were not paid promptly the loan might be called. This did not dovetail at all neatly with Ferdinand's plans to build himself and Hilda a new palace, acquire a luxurious private train, and purchase a yacht. Nevertheless, he went ahead with his plans; but to do so, he had to resort to methods that added nothing to his popularity, or perhaps it would be better to say, added considerably to his unpopularity.

Hilda had much more common sense than Ferdinand; but I don't know that that is particularly surprising, as I think that if the average gardener's daughter were stacked up against a run-of-mine king she would win out on that score nine times out of ten. She tried to advise Ferdinand.

"I do not think that you need a new palace, a train, or a yacht," she told him. "You already have this palace; I should be much happier back in my apartment; you have a comfortable private car that costs very little to maintain; and you can always charter a yacht when you want one, which is much cheaper than owning it. People are already commenting on your extravagances, which they blame on me. I am afraid something very terrible may happen, Ferdinand, if we are not more careful."

"You're just like the rest of them," he grumbled. "Nobody wants me to do anything that I want to do. Nobody seems to realize that I am the king and that I own this country and can do what I please with it. I'll show them."

* * * *

The cobbler's pretty daughter had been arrested after the assassination of Otto; and while they were questioning her she had learned all the details of that unhappy occurrence that the investigation had revealed, and suspected others that were ignored by the investigators. They did not hold her, as it was obvious that she had had no knowledge of the plot. To most of them she seemed only a dumb little girl of the lower classes, but to Captain Carlyn she seemed something more. She was a widow, and she was extremely pretty. Perhaps she would need a protector now that William had been taken from her. What neither Captain Carlyn nor the others realized was that the cobbler's pretty daughter was not as dumb as they thought her. During and after the investigation she did a great deal of thinking. She put two and two together, and was not at all surprised that they made neither three nor six; they made four, which bore out a theory she had been entertaining that William had been deliberately lured to his death for the purpose of diverting suspicion from the actual murderer of the King.

When she went home, she made inquiries among the friends and acquaintances of William; and visited places where she knew the radicals congregated to air their grievances against constituted authority. Among them, she was outspoken in her hatred of the King, whom she did not hate at all. She was playing a part, and she played it well. She made many strange friendships; and, because she was so pretty and seemed so dumb, men talked freely in front of her, thinking that she would not understand what they were talking about. She discovered that others believed as she did that William had been the victim of a plot to shield a higher-up; and what she learned from these men, added to what she had learned at the investigation, pointed indubitably to one man as the murderer of William; that he had also murdered the King was of no interest to the cobbler's pretty daughter. That was his business and the King's; but when a man kills a woman's mate, even such a poor specimen of a mate as William, that is something else.

After the investigation, Captain Carlyn sent for her several times. He spoke to her with sympathy and understanding, offering her financial assistance and any other help he could give her. She was very appreciative and very sweet, and further captivated him by her manner. So much so, in fact, that on a couple of occasions he almost forgot his role of fatherly concern and succumbed to a growing infatuation; but Captain Carlyn, being a soldier, was experienced in reducing fortresses, and knew that oftentimes to storm them prematurely is to suffer defeat.

After he was ordered to the frontier, he wrote to her, and she replied. Successive letters became more ardent, and the cobbler's daughter played up to him. Finally he sent for her, enclosing money for clothes and transportation.

TWENTY

To the south rode the galloping horseman until well out of sight of the douar. Then he turned abruptly to the west; and ever to his trail clung the tireless runner, lithe, agile, and swift.

Pig! Dog! Nameless vagabond! Nasrâny! All these appellations of reproach and shame surged through the memory of Azîz as he followed along the well-marked spoor.

Was it thus that he appeared in the eyes of Nakhla? Surely it must be, for all others looked down upon him.

Indeed he must be the lowest of Allah's creatures. Well, what he was, he was. He could not help nor alter it.

But if Nakhla looked down upon him why should he exert himself to rescue her from her abductors? He asked himself the question, realizing even as he put it that there was no need for it. His great love for the daughter of Ali-Es-Hadji was answer sufficient.

It was well toward noon that the trail led into a desolate and rocky gorge—granite bound, gloomy, and forbidding. In the depth of the narrow canyon Azîz went more slowly for there were many turns here, with rocky shoulders about which the spoor led. At any time he might round one of these obstacles and come full upon those he sought—it was the training of the wild beast that made him prefer to sneak stealthily along the spoor rather than to rush headlong—not through fear of personal danger, but lest the quarry, detecting him, might escape.

Azîz had advanced no great distance along the rocky defile when the report of a rifle shattered the sepulchral silence of the gorge, reverberating between its granite walls with a tumult that was appalling by contrast with the preceding quiet. Almost immediately this single shot was followed by another and another, until the sharp staccato of individual shots blended into the rattling legato of an almost continuous fusilade.

The lion-man, swiftly yet warily, pushed ahead until the rounding of a granite buttress disclosed to his view a widening of the canyon—a little flat amphitheater strewn with great boulders, and in the center of which was a small camp close beside a little well.

Half a dozen Arabs, evidently the owners of the camp, were firing from the cover of as many boulders upon an advancing troop of some twenty ill-favored tribesmen, who ran swiftly from the safety of one huge granite shelter to another as they crept closer and closer upon their intended victims.

That the attackers were of one of those roving bands of outlawed marauders which harass their more respectable brethren of the Sahara, Azîz guessed from his own experience with a similar gang at the time of his first meeting with Nakhla. Of the identity of the attacked he was not left long in doubt, for now, pressed closely by their enemies, they leaped to the backs of their snorting horses; amid a final volley of singing bullets and a rattle of stampeding hoofs, they galloped down the gorge, passing so close to the hidden lion-man that he easily recognized not only the messenger who had ridden into the douar of Ali-Es-Hadji that morning, but another as well—the solitary horseman who had brought him that last, blighting message from his Nakhla.

Instantly Azîz guessed that these were the men he sought—the scoundrels who had stolen Ali-Es-Hadji's daughter from her father's douar the night before; but first he wanted Nakhla—she must be rescued before ever he might indulge himself in the pleasure of revenge. His keen eyes searched the gorge ahead—nowhere was there sign of the presence of Nakhla. Where could she be? What fate had befallen her?

Beneath the boulder which hid Azîz from the galloping Arabs was a hole of sufficient depth to conceal him from anyone approaching from down the canyon. Into this the lion-man crept, so that when the marauders returning from the pursuit of the six who had escaped them passed this shelter they did not see him. Then he came stealthily out and followed them.

Neither threats nor pleas had availed Nakhla to release her from the clutches of Ben Saada. He had made

but a single promise—that she should be safe until the
messenger he had dispatched to her father had returned
with the answer of Sheik Ali-Es-Hadji. If the old man ac-
ceded to Ben Saada's demands they would at once return
to the douar where the marriage ceremony might be
regularly carried out after the custom of their tribe; but
if he did not—Ben Saada shrugged his shoulders as
though to say it was immaterial to him what the old
sheik's answer might be—he should have Nakhla in any
event.

At last they came into the little gorge far off the beaten
track of the caravan trails where Ben Saada felt that he
might safely hide pending the return of his messenger.
As they built their fires and drew water from the tiny well
in the cold hours of the waning night, none was aware
of the presence of another party of campers some fifty
yards above them, for the boulder-strewn ground might
have hid an army from the casual glances of a few un-
suspecting newcomers; but there were others there that
night within the gorge, nor were they ignorant of the
presence of the six Arab warriors and the girl. Keen eyes
had seen their coming long after keen ears had been
warned of the footsteps of their horses while still far down
the canyon.

Ben Saada and his little company lay down to sleep
after the leader had dispatched his message to Ali-Es-
Hadji. A single sleepy sentry stood upon watch, more to
prevent the escape of the girl than because of any fear
they entertained of the presence of enemies; and all the
while the fierce eyes of the savage marauders followed
every move within the camp of the newcomers.

Nakhla lay with closed eyes, feigning the regular
breathing of deep slumber, though never in her life had
she been so thoroughly awake. In her mind was the re-

solve to make a desperate break for liberty. There was no need to wait the return of the messenger—whatever the reply of her father, her fate was sealed unless she might find the means to win once more to the protection of her sire before Ben Saada should carry out his design upon her.

Below her stood the sentry. All but one of the other members of the party were stretched upon the ground between her and the direction she would have to take to return directly to her father's douar. To pass them all would be impossible, unless the sentry should sleep; but though Nakhla lay long waiting for slumber to overtake him, her eyes open now that the regular breathing of the men lying nearest her proclaimed that they slept, she discovered no indications that he ever would diminish his watchfulness, though for the most part he kept his gaze directed down the gorge, away from her.

Realizing at last that escape in this direction would be little short of impossible and that unless she acted quickly the coming dawn would preclude any attempt whatsoever, Nakhla at last determined upon the forlorn hope of making her way up the dark, forbidding gorge until she could find a place where she might scale its western wall and make her way back to the desert and the douar toward the north.

The distant roaring of lions sent both a tremor of nervous terror through the girl and a sudden longing for the happy days that she had spent with her Azîz, and his great brother, el adrea. The thought of the man brought also a quick tightening of the lips and a clenching of the slim, brown hands—jealousy, green-eyed and blighting, clutched her fast-beating heart. She saw as plainly as though they stood before her now, the handsome, khaki-clad white man sitting his horse beside the laughing girl of his own color—ah, that was the misery of it—a girl of his own color. For the first time in her life Nakhla hated the beautiful bronze of her own smooth skin.

But now there was no time for such thoughts or such repining. The dangerous business of the minute must be done now or never. Cautiously the girl slipped from the rug that covered her. The sentry still stood like a graven image, his face turned toward the north. Upon her hands and knees Nakhla crept around the form of a single sleeper who lay a few yards above her. The man moved, throwing an arm above his head; and the girl halted, frozen to terrified silence. Then he breathed again with the quiet regularity of deep slumber.

On she went. Now she was beyond them all. A great boulder loomed dark before her. Behind it she would rest for a moment and quiet her shaken nerves. As she moved, a score of eyes watched her from up the canyon. They saw her come in safety to the great boulder and hide there for a moment. They saw her resume her stealthy way upward directly toward them.

When Nakhla resumed her flight after a momentary pause behind the first boulder she came to her feet, for now she could keep the great rock between herself and Ben Saada's camp. She moved more swiftly now but still taking advantage of every cover, running quickly from behind one huge granite fragment to the screening safety of the next.

Thus she made her way for fifty yards, when, coming about the shoulder of another shelter, she ran straight into the arms of a man who closed with her, clapping a great hand over her mouth. A moment later she was surrounded by others of her own race.

Grimly they warned her to silence, leading her far up the canyon to where were others holding horses as though ready for instant flight. Here she remained under a strong guard, and with the rising of the sun she saw from the appearance of her captors that she had at last fallen into the hands of such a band of marauders as her Azîz had preserved her from upon that first day of their friendship.

She could not guess the purpose of the long wait under the hot sun, and to all her questions her guards returned only sullen scowls. It was about noon that she heard a rattle of musketry far down the gorge, the sound of firing diminished in the distance as the combatants moved down the tight little canyon.

Half an hour later the main body of the marauders returned hot and dusty. They were very angry—their prey had escaped them. Their leader had guessed from what Nakhla had told him that Ben Saada's messenger had gone forth to demand ransom for the girl and it was with the hope of securing this should the man have been successful in obtaining it that they had waited and watched in the gorge for the return of the messenger.

Now they were wroth indeed, and black and ugly were the looks they cast upon the girl, as though it was she who had caused them to lose the ransom money they had hoped to obtain. She heard them arguing among themselves with occasional glances in her direction which indicated quite plainly the subject of their debate.

It was evident that some sood out for one plan while others adhered tenaciously to another; but at last a tall, brutal-looking fellow who seemed to be the leader decided the matter peremptorily, and with a few orders to his followers rose from the council, coming over to where Nakhla sat with her back to a large boulder.

"Get up," he said, gruffly. "You will ride behind Mohammed," and he nodded toward the sentry.

"Where are you taking me?" asked Nakhla.

"Where you will fetch a good price," and he nodded toward the south.

Nakhla understood. "Why not go at once to Ali-Es-Hadji," she said, "and have thy foul heart cut out, for sooner or later the sheik, my father, will find you and avenge his daughter."

The man grinned. "Ali-Es-Hadji will ride far before he comes upon Sidi-El-Seghir," he replied. "I know the old wolf well enough to keep far from his country after robbing him of his whelp."

"All Africa will hold no corner far enough from his wrath that you may escape it," said Nakhla.

Sidi-El-Seghir scowled. He was much of the same opinion himself, but he cared not to hear his fears voiced by another.

"Then," continued Nakhla, "there are the French. The Sultan has given them permission to build a fort by the caravan route close to the sea. Already they have made friends with Sheik Ali-Es-Hadji. He will go to them, and they will help him find you—the arm of the white man is long, Sidi-El-Seghir. They will surely get you before you can dispose of me."

"Then," said Sidi-El-Seghir, "we must waste no time here. Come," and turning to his followers he issued such commands as were necessary to set the band of ruffians upon their way, Nakhla riding behind Mohammed's saddle.

Straight up the narrow gorge they filed, passing out of it by a steep and rocky path to a rough upland country across which travelling was arduous and slow; and behind them moved a beast of prey, taking advantage of every cover, his fierce eyes fixed upon the girl who rode among her captors.

In his haste Sidi-El-Seghir mistook the way, so that

late afternoon found him and his party in a little cul-de-sac in the mountains, from which there was no way out other than that which required the retracting of their steps for a matter of a two-hour march or more.

It was getting late; and so the marauder decided to camp where he was for the night, for here at least was water, whereas, should he go back to take up the right trail at the point at which they had left it, they should have to make a dry camp that night.

Above them, prowling along the rim of the encircling cliffs, moved the beast that had stalked them all afternoon. He saw Sidi-El-Seghir place a guard at the narrow mouth of the little, rocky pocket in which the marauders were preparing camp. He could not pass in that way without being detected, for the entrance was scarce three feet wide, passing between the narrow walls where they almost came together; and directly in the narrowest part the sentry was posted.

But over the precipitous edge there might be a way, and it was in search of such that the beast prowled back and forth until long after dusk had fallen. In the gathering shadows he twice essayed the descent, but in each instance found insufficient foothold to permit him to reach the bottom in safety. Each time he carefully retraced his steps to the summit to renew the attempt at another point.

Below, in the camp, the Arabs ate—a few handfuls of dried dates, following a scanty ration of beans cooked above a tiny sagebrush fire. For half an hour thereafter they kept the fire burning while they smoked and talked; then, rolling themselves up in their rugs, they stretched out about the glowing embers of the dying blaze to sleep.

Nakhla lay a little apart from her captors turning over in her active mind a score of possibilities for escape or rescue. She knew that Ali-Es-Hadji would lose no time in taking up the pursuit of her abductors, but whether he would be able to follow their spoor over the rough and rocky trail that they had followed for so considerable a part of the flight she doubted.

In her thoughts, too, came the memory of the tall and handsome brother of el adrea. Now, perhaps, he was sitting at the feet of the French girl, even as he had sat at her feet, stroking the white hand of the stranger. Nakhla's breast rose and fell in riotous jealousy and hate.

"The Nasrâny!" she muttered. "I hate him!" and then out of the darkness, close behind her she heard the low purring of a lion.

Startled, Nakhla came to her elbow. Her lips had formed a cry of warning to the Arabs, when, whispered in a scarce audible breath from the point in the darkness upon which her terrified eyes were riveted, there issued a low: "Nakhla!"

The Nasrâny! I hate him. The words that she formed inaudibly a moment before came rushing back from her memory. She needed no confirming proof of sight to know that it was he—the Nasrâny.

A moment later he was beside her. The Arabs, deep in slumber, were insensible to the silent tread of the lion-man. The sentry was too far away to have heard even a much noiser approach.

"Come!" he said, and taking her by the hand led softly toward the overhanging cliff upon the west side of the basin.

As they left, Sidi-El-Seghir stirred in his sleep. Some presentiment of wrong awakened him. He sat up, rubbing his eyes and peering about him through the darkness. There was no sound. All seemed quite as it should be. He was about to settle down once more, when the insist-

ence of the apprehension that something was afoot that
boded him ill altered his intention. It would do no harm
to have a look at the prisoner.

Rising, Sidi-El-Seghir strode to the spot where Nakhla
had placed the dirty rug they had loaned her. She was
gone! Instantly the marauder's voice rang out upon the
silence of the wilderness. His men sprang to their feet.

"The girl!" he cried. "She has gone! Make a light and
search for her."

Then he ran to where the sentry stood. She could not
have passed him, the fellow swore by Allah and His
prophet.

"She must then be still within the basin," said Sidi-El-
Seghir, "unless, dog, thou hast slept," but the sentry insisted that he had not closed an eye, and so the leader
and his motley crew of ruffians set to work over every
inch of the small cul-de-sac.

Near the westward cliff Azîz was searching for the
meager foothold that had given him ingress to the basin
from that side. With one hand he grasped the hand of
Nakhla, and with the other groped about the cliff's steep
face, peering through the darkness for the way he had
come. Neither had spoken—the enemy were too close at
hand. They could now hear the voice of Sidi-El-Seghir
raised angrily.

Gradually the darkness of the pit-like place was lifting
before the moon which slowly rose above the eastern
wall. The Arab leader had sage brush piled upon the
embers of the dying fire to light up the surroundings in
the hope that the whereabouts of the girl might be revealed. Already the flames were leaping higher and higher, but it was the moon the fugitives need fear the most.

A dozen times Azîz attempted to scale the steep cliff,
only to be baffled by some overhanging crag ere he had

gained a score of upward feet. Now the Arabs were spreading out over the entire area of the basin. In the growing light of the fire, Azîz and Nakhla could see them, and then the moon topped the eastern barrier flooding the face of the westward cliff in its soft light.

Clear cut and distinct against the bare rock the figures of the man and the maid stood cut as though a searchlight had been turned upon them. Instantly there was a shout of savage relief from the marauders, as they raced toward the two.

Azîz had left his musket, bandoleer, pistol and knife at the cliff top. Naked but for his loin cloth he had made the descent, for he could not risk the chance alarm of an accouterment scraping upon the rocky wall.

Now, as the Arabs charged, the lion-man crouched. For all the world he looked to the girl at his side like a lion at bay. His eyes flamed, his head was flattened, his fine, strong lips were slightly upcurved to expose the fighting fangs, and from his deep throat rumbled the angry challenge of el adrea.

Before his menacing attitude and hideous growls the armed men halted looking wonderingly at him and at one another.

"It is the same," cried Sidi-El-Seghir, "that attacked us with el adrea when Kaliphe would have taken this same girl and was killed by this beast-man."

"Allah!" exclaimed another. "It is no man—it is a devil. Let us hasten away."

But idi-El-Seghir had gone too far now to be thwarted by either man or devil, and so with leveled musket he advanced upon the naked man, calling to his companions to do likewise.

With a score of firearms aimed directly at them, Nakhla realized that all thoughts of escape or even resistance must be foregone. She did not wish to see her would-be rescuer slain as the sole reward for having championed her. She laid a cool hand upon his shoulder.

"There is no use," she said. "Let us give ourselves up now, and await another opportunity."

But scarce had she voiced the plea when Azîz sprang for the nearest Arab. The fellow's matchlock missed fire, and then he was down beneath rending fangs. His companions dared not fire for fear of hitting him, but they clubbed their guns and a moment later it was an insensible lion-man that lay securely bound beside the fire. At his head sat Nakhla bathing the wound upon his forehead.

TWENTY-ONE

Seven men were gathered in the back room of the little inn with which we are familiar. There were two former officers of The Guards Regiment, who had just been transferred to the frontier regiment; there were two officers of the Seventh Regiment of Infantry, and two from the Tenth Cavalry Regiment; the seventh man was Andresy.

"The people are ripe for revolt," said Andresy. "Increased taxation has fallen heavily on all classes. If the money were to be spent for the public good, they might forgive it; but it is to be spent for a new palace, a private train, a yacht, and the extravagant private life of the King and his—associates." A lieutenant of the 10th Cavalry flushed and looked straight ahead. "The situation is intolerable, and the people are furious."

"The restlessness had spread to the army also," said

one of the officers. "He has transferrred many officers of The Guards to regiments stationed on the frontier, replacing them by his friends and those of Lomsk. He has raised the pay of The Guards and cut that of every other branch of the service, rank and file as well as officers. I think that we can now work together."

"Our interests are mutual," said Andresy. "We do not ask much—merely the formation of a republic and the adoption of the new liberal constitution. We wouldn't even ask for a republic, if there were any member of the royal family acceptable to the people for accession to the throne; but there is not. In the new government, it has been suggested that General Count Sarnya represent the army, and I, the people. Is that satisfactory to you gentlemen?" His eyes searched the faces of the six.

"It is," said he who spoke for the officers. "Sarnya is loved by the army. He holds it in the hollow of his hand. There could be no better man than he."

"Will he work with us?" asked Andresy. "He has been a staunch monarchist all his life, you know."

"I have spoken to him within the week," replied the officer. "He will support any move to rid the country of Ferdinand."

"Good," said Andresy. "The details of the coup I shall leave to you gentlemen. I am sure that you are far more capable of handling it than I; but please keep me informed—I should like to know the exact day and hour that you intend to strike."

"General Sarnya has applied for leave, which has been granted; and he will arrive in the capital next Thursday," said the officer.

"The next day is Friday the thirteenth," said Lieutenant Hans de Groot.

"An excellent date," commented Andresy; "one that will always be easy to remember. Do you know the hour?"

"Three o'clock in the morning," replied Lieutenant de Groot.

* * * *

"They started pouring the foundations for the palace this morning," said the King. "I am having a little silver casket made to place beneath the corner stone when I lay it; it will contain nothing but a lock of your hair."

" 'Casket'!" repeated Hilda, with a shudder. "I do not like the word."

Ferdinand laughed. "Well, we shall call it a box, then."

Hilda did not laugh. "When I drove today, some people hissed me; when I passed the cemetery, I saw a man digging a grave. Oh, Ferdinand, send for Maria; and let me go back to my apartment. We were so happy before, and nobody seemed really to mind—nobody but Hans. Poor Hans!"

"I am going to make him a general," said Ferdinand, "and then he will be happy; and I have a surprise for you, too, my dear."

"What is it? No more jewels, I hope. There is always some nasty little squib in the Paris papers every time you give me anything."

"I am going to create you a countess," said Ferdinand. "Then they cannot say that I married a commoner after I divorce Maria."

Hilda shook her head. "You are very sweet, Ferdinand; but you are also very blind and foolish. Even if I were Queen, I should always be a gardener's daughter to *them*. I wish you would not do it."

"I shall, though," he said, stubbornly. "I am king, and I shall do as I please."

* * * *

The cobbler's pretty daughter arrived at the frontier on Wednesday, the eleventh. She had enjoyed the trip by train very much indeed, because she had never been on a train before and because this was the farthest she had ever been from home. She felt quite travelled and cosmopolitan. She also enjoyed the trip because of the smart, new clothes she had bought with the money Captain Carlyn had sent her—the kind and generous Captain Carlyn. She knew how to dress, because she had worked in a swank modiste's shop in the capital before she and William had married; and she could wear clothes, because —well, just because she could wear them. It is a knack that one is born with, or isn't—most people are not.

When Captain Carlyn met her at the train, he was very proud of her, indeed. He thought that she was quite the loveliest thing he had ever seen; and in that he was, perhaps, quite right. He congratulated himself upon his good taste and his good fortune. He took her to a hotel, where she registered; and then he took her to lunch. He was very attentive—very much the enamored lover. That afternoon he paraded her through the little frontier town, eliciting envious glances from fellow officers. They dined together late that night; and then they went to her room. After they entered it, Captain Carlyn turned and locked the door leading into the corridor.

* * * *

On that same Wednesday, Hans de Groot went to see his mother and father. They talked of the army and of politics and the nursery business, of everything except that which was on their minds, for Hans had not spoken Hilda's name to his parents for years. Finally Martin de Groot had to leave to look over a job his men were working on. After he had gone, Hans knelt on the floor and buried his head in his mother's lap. She ran her fingers through his hair and stroked his head. Finally he turned his face so that he could speak. "I have been thinking of Michael so much of late," he said. "What good times we used to have—Michael and Hilda and I." He had spoken her name at last. After that it was easier. He recalled little incidents of their childhood. Now he could talk of nothing else but Hilda. But he never spoke of Ferdinand or any other unpleasant thing. When it came time for him to go, he held his mother very tight and kissed her many times. She felt his tears on her face.

TWENTY-TWO

After Azîz had left them in the canyon of their lair, the lion and the lioness roamed restlessly about for an hour or two, returning about dawn to the carcass of a buck they had killed the previous day, where they ate for a while. Then they went down to the river and drank, splashing the cool water noisily. For a few minutes they stood looking up and down the canyon; then the lion turned up toward their den, and followed by his savage mate crept in and lay down.

It was dusk again before either stirred. The lioness rose first and yawned, stretching her great length. The lion, aroused, opened his yellow eyes and stared up at his mate. She purred down upon him. Slowly and majestically the king of beasts came to his feet. As he passed his lioness his rough tongue stroked her muzzle in a gentle caress, and a moment later his massive head and great black mane were framed in the entrance of the cave.

With slow, ponderous dignity the huge beast strode out

into the growing night. He moved noisily down the narrow trail toward the canyon's bottom, at his heels his fond companion. Occasionally the great head turned toward the right or toward the left, but there was no stealth in his movements, and no sign of that nervous trepidation which marks the waking life of the lesser beasts of the wilderness. What need of caution upon the part of the lord of the desert! Only when he would hunt did he send his great, sinuous frame through tangled grasses or dense brush in utter noiselessness.

At the river the two drank. Then they turned their footsteps toward the remains of their kill. They were travelling upwind, when to their sensitive nostrils came the scent of flesh. It was an unwary antelope drinking fifty yards above them.

As by magic the two great cats became silent spectres moving through the gloomy shadows of the canyon. The lion was in advance. As he crept forward his huge padded feet gave no slightest warning of his coming. Not a grass blade rustled. Not a twig snapped beneath his noiseless tread. Eight hundred pounds, perhaps, the great beast weighed, yet no tit-mouse could have moved in silence more complete.

Almost to the drinking antelope he came before that nervous, fearful creature sensed anything amiss, even then it heard no noise. Some subtle sense of peril brought its horned head aloft and alert, but too late.

With a blood-curdling roar el adrea hurtled from the bush at its side. With a frantic snort the creature wheeled to fly, but a might taloned forepaw, swinging with all the terrific force of a steam hammer fell upon its shoulder. The bone shattered beneath that awful blow, and then gleaming fangs were buried in the soft throat. There was scarce a struggle after that.

Neatly the lion tore open the body of his kill and disemboweled it. The entrails he buried on the spot, amidst much roaring and growling. Then he grasped the carcass by the face and dragged it fifty or sixty yards to a little clump of bushes, where, purring and grunting, he and his lioness filled their bellies.

As they ate, the clatter of hoofs fell upon their ears from down the canyon. The two waited, crouching behind their kill, their heads flattened and their eyes gleaming like coals of fire. Presently there came within their view a party of horsemen—fifty perhaps. They wore the khaki of European soldiery—all but one, and he rode, white burnoosed, at the head of the column beside the leader of the troop. He was Ali-Es-Hadji's messenger bringing Colonel Vivier and a detail of troopers to assist the Arab in the recovery of his daughter.

The party rode by within fifty yards of the two lions without seeing them. When they had passed, the male rose and looked after them. Then he commenced pacing restlessly about sniffing the ground. It was here that they had pounced upon their brother last night. It was here that he had bid them goodbye and gone away in the direction in which all these men were now riding.

What passed within the fierce, tawny head? Who may guess? He came close to the side of his lioness, sniffing and whining. At last she, too, came to her feet, and then commenced a restless pacing such as one sees within the barred prison cages of the zoo. Back and forth the mighty beasts of prey strode, until at the last the lion, raising his huge head, gave voice to an angry challenging roar, and with tail up set out at a rapid trot upon the trail of the horsemen, and at his heels followed his lioness.

Before they had emerged from the canyon the trot had slackened to a walk, and after that they moved easily, with great strides, over the hills and out into the desert—two mighty creatures of destruction, upon what errand? moved by what promptings?

All that night they traveled, lying up for a few hours during the heat of the following day, for lions though they can cover great distances without fatigue in the cool of the darkness suffer greatly under a scorching sun.

During the second night they passed through a narrow rocky gorge, and out of it up a steep cliff side that must have taxed the endurance of the horses that preceded them.

Close to dawn they came upon a camp in which were many men sleeping. Great fires burned, and all about stood a thin line of watchful humans, leaning upon their long black guns.

The lions skulked through the surrounding darkness, circling the camp a dozen times, and making a night hideous for the sentries with their uncanny "Aà—ows," and deep, solemn "Goom! Goom!"

Whatever they searched for they did not find; and before the camp, which consisted of Colonel Vivier's men and Ali-Es-Hadji's warriors, broke in the early morning the lions were far in advance of them upon another spoor. This time it was a definite spoor which they had recognized and could follow.

When Azîz regained consciousness he was aware principally of a severe ache in his head. As he opened his eyes, Nakhla ceased to bathe his forehead. He looked up at her and smiled—it was a smile that reminded her of the smile that he had turned upon the white Nasrâny girl. With the memory came flooding back all the embittered, jealous anguish that she had suffered because of it, and which had been almost forgotten during the vigil at the side of the wounded man.

The turned her eyes haughtily away, and then rising walked to a little distance and stood with her back toward him. For a long time his gaze remained fixed upon her unbending and relentless figure.

"Nasrâny," he thought. "Pig. Dog." No wonder that she did not care to look at him, and then he sighed and turned upon his face, burying his hurting head in his arms.

At dawn the marauders were ready to break camp. Several of them were for making short work of the brother of el adrea; but for some reason of his own, Sidi-El-Seghir preferred to spare the prisoner's life for a while. Perchance he anticipated a price for so powerfully built a slave at the court of the lazy black sultan to the south.

The day was yet in its infancy when the Arabs took up their march. It was not yet precisely flight, for they did not guess that so large a force was upon their trail, but Sidi-El-Seghir was endowed with sufficient wisdom to guess that Ali-Es-Hadji would not permit his daughter to be thus boldly stolen and make no strenuous effort to succor her; so he pushed on at as good a pace as the rough country permitted.

Nakhla rode upon the rump of Mohammed's mount; but Azîz, a stout camel hair rope about his neck, was tethered to the saddle of Sidi-El-Seghir. There was little ground across which the horses could move faster than a walk; but even where they went at a trot or a canter for short distances the lion-man found less difficulty in keeping the pace than did the wiry beasts the Arabs rode.

The prisoner's agility and endurance so greatly interested Sidi-El-Seghir that he became more than ever determined to carry the captive with him—the price that he had placed upon him growing steadily with the rough miles the almost naked white man covered without apparent exertion or fatigue.

During the long, hot day Azîz was aware of but two things—the terrible hurting in his head and the cold, disdainful glances of the girl whom the accidents of the march occasionally brought close to him. It was difficult to say which caused the keenest anguish.

Night found them far to the south, yet still clinging to the eastern side of the foothills; though the traveling was difficult there was more cover, and water permitted of easier marches. Here, in a hollow, they halted for the night.

Azîz hoped for a word with Nakhla then, that he might learn for truth if it were his low estate that lay at the bottom of her aloofness; but try as he would he could get no speech with her, and at last when he saw that she had rolled herself up in her rug for the night he lay down beside the guard to whom he was tied, and tried to efface his suffering in sleep.

For half the night he tossed and turned upon the hard ground. His captors had given him no covering, but he did not suffer much on this account though he would have been glad of the soft, hot body of el adrea against which he had snuggled on so many countless nights.

Even as he thought of the great beast there came faintly to him the distant "Goom! Goom!" of a lion. Ah, if it were but his own loved companion! But there could be no hope of that—too far from the haunts of his savage chum had the Arabs dragged him.

As he lay listening to the sound that fell so sweetly upon his ears, another impinged upon his sensitive perceptions—the muffled fall of iron-shod hoofs upon the rock trail along which they had come that day. All his faculties were awake now. The awful torture of his wounded skull was all but forgotten. Motionless as death he listened intently, for he knew that the iron shoes meant the soldiery of France. What could they be doing upon this trail? Yet it must be they, and with them would come rescue for his Nakhla. He did not think of himself. He did not care other than for the welfare of her around whom the mantle of his love would drape its protecting folds.

Closer and closer came the sound of the approaching horsemen, until he wondered at the deafness of the sentries who showed no sign of having heard the noise which fell upon his sensitive ears with such distinctness.

Presently the sound ceased, to be followed by that of the stealthy creeping of an individual toward the camp. Nearer and nearer it came. At last the sentries awoke to the nearness of an enemy. A musket flashed and roared, to be answered from the stunted bush beyond the camp by another.

Instantly the bivouac was astir. Arabs sprang armed and ready to repel the attack they had known must come sooner or later. Matchlocks bellowed and spit great sheets of fire into the dark belly of the night.

Sidi-El-Seghir dragged Nakhla to the shelter of a large boulder. Then he summoned Mohammed to fetch Azîz to the same point and watch over them.

"Should they attempt to escape, shoot them," commanded the marauder, and ran forward to take his place upon the firing line, prone behind a rocky shelter.

Now there came the sharp, clear-cut ping of the white man's rifle. It was followed by a volley, perfectly delivered, that revealed to Sidi-El-Seghir the straits into which he had blundered. It was bad enough to have Ali-Es-Hadji hunting him down, but with the force of the white man's arm beside him the marauder's position was far from enviable.

The night was yet very dark. The moon had not risen. Stealthily Sidi-El-Seghir slunk back to the boulder which sheltered Mohammed and the two prisoners. He found another Arab there who evidently had no stomach for the bullets of the white man.

"Come!" whispered Sidi-El-Seghir. "The others will hold off the foe while we carry the prisoners to safety." He did not mention that the others knew nothing of his plan.

Behind the camp were the horses. Their guard had run forward to join the fighting at the front. Quickly the three Arabs saddled their beasts, and with Azîz walking and strapped to Sidi-El-Seghir's saddle bow and Nakhla mounted behind Mohammed, the fugitives broke straight up into the wild, rough going of the hills. Here, surely, thought Sidi-El-Seghir, he should lose the white man and possibly obtain sufficient start of Ali-Es-Hadji to make good his escape to the wild country through which no man could trail him.

Below them they heard the rattle of the musketry, the crieds and cursings of the wounded, and the occasional shriek of a mortally hit horse. It was a hot battle, hotly waged. Sidi-El-Seghir was not sorry that he had escaped it. Ambush and murder were more in his line than open fighting, man to man.

As they reached a little tableland Azîz heard again the roaring of a lion, but this time it was much closer—coming apparently from directly behind them out of the black abyss through which they had climbed to the moonlight mesa. He thrilled to the savage notes.

The Arabs heard them, too, and pressed forward as rapidly as possible. At times the gait taxed even the magnificent speed of the lion-man, but he was buoyed by a strange hope that filled his breast. Could it be that he had recognized the fierce notes of his brother in the voice of the beast upon their trail?"

His keen ears detected the closer grunting of the beast as it approached and finally paralleled them. Presently he was aware that there were two of them, and once he caught the sheen of their tawny hides as they passed from cover to cover a hundred yards to the right. No, there could be no mistake. How his heart leaped as hope grew almost to certainty.

The Arabs were now aware of the presence of the lions. Constantly their eyes were turned fearfully toward those two grim shadows that loped so silently upon their flank.

"Hasten!" muttered Sidi-El-Seghir. "The brutes will be upon us if we do not distance them soon." But the way was too rough for the jaded horses to better their speed.

Presently the party broke out upon a smooth and open, park-like space. The brilliant moon flooded the scene with light. Sidi-El-Seghir looked fearfully toward the huge beasts that seemed so horribly close.

He could see their jaws drooping open and the light flashing upon their white fangs. The Arab shuddered. Mohammed breathed a little prayer to Allah and drove his spurs into his horse's sides. Nakhla looked apprehensively toward the lions and then at Azîz. Could these be his beasts? And if they were, could they know him and her so far from their own environment?

The lion and his mate were drawing imperceptibly closer with each stride—edging in toward the little party of horsemen. Sidi-El-Seghir raised his ancient matchlock to fire from the back of his galloping horse. But even as his finger tightened upon the trigger a sudden skirring growl broke from the lips of a beast at his side.

Startled, the Arab glanced down to see the tethered white man leaping upward toward him with outstretched hands. Could that bestial sound have risen from a human throat? For answer he saw the lips part to a hideous roar, and even as he clubbed his rifle to beat off the creature threatening him he felt the sinewy fingers at his shoulder. The man had leaped to his side and was dragging him down even as a beast of prey drags down its quarry.

As he fell he heard the horrid roaring of the two lions mingling with the snarls of his own antagonist, and caught a fleeting glimpse of the tawny bodies charging down upon the party.

Then the teeth of the lion-man found his throat and Sidi-El-Seghir's ghost glided fearfully out of the wilderness of Africa into the unknown.

TWENTY-THREE

When Hans de Groot came to mess for breakfast on Thursday, the twelfth, he found his fellow officers in a state of mild excitement.

"Your friend, Carlyn, was killed last night," said one of them. "Here it is in the morning paper. He was shot by a woman in her room in a hotel on the frontier."

Hans took the paper and read the brief article. "Wesl," he said; "why that was the name of the fellow who assassinated the King. They must have been a very dangerous couple. Well, she will hang for it; and that will be the end of both of them."

"I am a great believer in capital punishment," said another officer. "People who commit murders should die."

"Yes," agreed Hans.

General Count Sarnya arrived in the capital in the afternoon and had an immediate audience with the King. Ferdinand was cold and arrogant. He had always hated Sarnya, probably because Sarnya was a strong character and a very popular man. Ferdinand was neither. He mistook stubbornness for strength, and depended upon his power and his title for popularity.

"Conditions are very bad, Your Majesty," said Sarnya. "There is a great deal of unrest. The people need only a spark to set them off. The army cannot be depended upon. I beg of you to make a gesture of conciliation at once—today. If you will announce that you will accept the new constitution and at the same time restore the former pay to all grades in the services, I am positive that you will forestall a disaster."

"I did not send for you to ask your advice," said Ferdinand, coldly. "I sent for you to tell you to prepare the frontier forces for war. I am going to march on the capital of my father-in-law, and teach the old fool a lesson. When I get through with him, the indemnity he'll have to pay will more than wipe out the loan he has had the effrontery to call."

General Count Sarnya stood very straight before the King. "I have warned you, Ferdinand," he said, "just as I warned your uncle many years ago. Because he was a great king and a very brave man, he chose to ignore my warning. You are ignoring it because you are a fool. Let the consequences be on your own head."

Ferdinand jumped to his feet, trembling with rage. "How dare you speak to me like that?" he demanded. "You are under arrest. We shall know what to do with traitors."

Sarnya laughed at him. "You cannot arrest me," he

179

said. "At a word from me the whole army would rise against you, and you know it"; then he turned on his heel and quit the room.

Ferdinand sank back in his chair, still trembling.

* * * *

"Hilda," said Ferdinand, "have your maid pack a bag and get your wraps; we are going to the hunting lodge for a few days. I am sick and tired of all the wrangling and dissension here. I want a rest."

"Why, Ferdinand, it's after midnight," objected Hilda, "and I'm tired. I want to go to bed."

"You can sleep better out there in the woods, and it doesn't take long to drive out. Come on."

"No; it's Friday the thirteenth; and I wouldn't start anywhere on that date," said Hilda. "We'll go Saturday."

"Oh, very well; have your own way," snapped Ferdinand, petulantly.

* * * * *

When Friday morning dawned, the streets of the capital were filled with soldiers. They surrounded the palace and all the government buildings and the national bank. There were barricades and machine guns across many of the principal streets. General Count Sarnya was in command.

Rumors flew thick and fast. The people were nervous and terrified. No newspapers had been issued. There was tenseness in the air. At last an official bulletin was issued announcing that a state of martial law existed. It also told briefly the occurrences of the early hours of the morning of Friday the thirteenth.

"At three o'clock in the morning," it stated, "six officers forced their way into the palace and the King's apartments. There they found and killed both the King and Mademoiselle de Groot. Lieutenant Hans de Groot, who was one of the six officers involved, shot himself through the head immediately following the death of his sister; he died instantly."

TWENTY-FOUR

Mohammed and the other Arab, terror-stricken upon their terror-stricken mounts, attempted to escape. The former to lighten the burden upon his horse turned in his saddle and pushed Nakhla to the ground; but it was too late. The girl saw a flash of leaping, white fanged rage spring for the rider. A mighty, taloned paw raked the Arab from the horse's back; great jaws closed upon his head; and then the lion gave the limp form a vicious shake and dropped it.

The other Arab, a few yards in advance as he had been, was able to make good his escape, for the lions had attacked upon rather level, open ground where the advantage was all upon the side of the fleet horses. Now the lioness was returning at a quick trot toward her mate.

Nakhla looked about her. The lion stood scarce ten feet from her, his yellow eyes fixed full upon her. Behind him the lioness was approaching. A hundred feet to one side Azîz was just rising from the body of Sidi-El-Seghir. He could not reach her ahead of the lions. Would the black-maned one remember her?

The same question rose in the mind of the man, and with great leaps he hastened toward the girl, shouting at the same time to the lions. The lioness had now come to a halt just behind her mate, where she, too, stood eyeing the girl and growling savagely.

The lion advanced slowly toward Nakhla. The girl stood quietly with extended hand, speaking to the great brute as she had been wont to do when she and Azîz and el adrea had lolled through hot afternoons beneath the shade of some great tree beside the little river in their own beloved canyon.

The huge beast was close before her when he halted, and raising his muzzle rubbed it beneath her palm—begging for a caress. It was with a sigh of relief that was almost a sob that the girl dropped to her knees and threw both arms about the savage, black-maned neck. Behind them the lioness growled questioningly, and then Azîz leaped to her side.

It did not take the lioness long to learn that Nakhla was one of them—that she must not be harmed, though for a while the lion or the man kept always between them.

When Nakhla came to her feet she saw Azîz looking down upon her, with a deep sadness that she never before had seen upon his countenance. She had been minded to thank him for his protection and then turn her back upon him; but there was that in his face that made her forget even the white girl—his wife.

"What is it?" she whispered. "Are you in pain?—does the wound upon your head still cause you suffering?"

He looked at her for a moment in dumb misery. The pain in his head was almost intolerable.

"It is not my head that hurts, Nakhla," he said, and he laid his hand upon his heart—"it is here that the hurt is."

"I do not understand," she answered. "I thought that you were very happy—you seemed so when you rode to my father's douar beside the white girl."

"How could the brother of el adrea be happy," he asked, "knowing that Nakhla was wed to another?"

" 'Nakhla wed to another'?" she cried. "What do you mean?"

"Did you not send a messenger out into the desert to tell me that I must come no more to visit you—that you were married to a man of your own tribe?"

Instantly the girl read the truth.

"Ben Saada!" she exclaimed. "None but Ben Saada would have done so vile a thing."

"It is not true, then?" he cried, his voice trembling.

"It is not true, Azîz," she answered. "Nakhla is wed to no man."

The use of the name that she had given him, and that he had not heard upon her lips for so long sent a thrill through him. He came close to her side.

"I know now what 'azîz' means," he said.

Nakhla flushed, and at the same instant she thought of what Ben Saada had told her—that this man was married to the white girl of the French. She drew quickly away from him.

"Nakhla is not married," she said, speaking quickly, "but can the brother of el adrea say the same for himself?"

"You know, Nakhla," he answered simply, "that I am not wed to you, and so I cannot be wed to any."

"But the French girl?" she asked, still in doubt.

Azîz laughed.

"She was like a sister to me, who had never had a sister. How could I, having seen Nakhla, love any other upon the face of the earth?"

This last argument seemed to be quite convincing; and Nakhla came close to him, looking up into his face.

Still he did not take her in his arms, though that is precisely what Nakhla wished him to do. In a moment she was piqued. Her eyes flashed and her chin took upon itself the haughty tilt that made her lips seem irresistible.

Azîz was moved, but he could not forget that he was a Nasrâny, a pig, a dog of an unbeliever, everything in fact that was low and despicable in the eyes of Arab or white.

The firing behind them—the guns of the allies against the marauders—had long since ceased; but neither had noted the fact, nor in truth anything other than one another. The moon stood directly above them, and a few paces away the lion and the lioness tore at the flesh of Mohammed's horse, for the animal had been crippled by the same mighty blow that had swept his rider to death.

"Come," said Nakhla, coldly. "Back there are my people. I am going to them. The Sheik Ali-Es-Hadji, my father, will repay you for that which you have done in the service of his daughter."

"Pay!" exclaimed Azîz. Why should you hurt me more by saying such a thing as that? Is it not enough that so low a one as I dare love all hopelessly such as you, that you must add hurt to my sorrow by suggesting that I could take pay for servicing you?"

Nakhla looked straight into the eyes of the lion-man. "I do not know," she said, "what you mean by saying that you are 'low.' Nor can I guess any more what your sentiments may be—I have seen no indications of love. Perhaps the lion-man is not so brave as a lion, after all." There was a diabolical little smile of mischief upon her lips.

Azîz, dense as most men are in the matter of a maid's love, awoke at last from his stupid lethargy. Before she could have prevented had she desired to do so he had sezied her, and when she found herself crushed to his broad breast her hands stole up about his neck and slowly drew his lips downward upon hers.

It was upon this scene that two men looked—a French Colonel and an Arab Sheik. They had topped a little rise of ground as it broke upon their startled visions, bringing them to a sudden halt within the concealing fringe of bush through which they had been riding.

"Allah!" exclaimed the Arab. "Look!"

"Mon dieu!" ejaculated Colonel Vivier. "See those great lions feeding behind them—it is incredible."

"The lion-man—and my daughter," whispered Ali-Es-Hadji, half to himself.

"And you really love me?" Azîz was asking. "You do not think that I am a pig or a dog or any of the other things that men call me?"

"I love you," whispered the girl. "You are Azîz, Nakhla's azîz."

And again he crushed her close to him, covering her faces with kisses.

Sheik Ali-Es-Hadji saw, and groaned.

"The dog!" he muttered.

Colonel Vivier looked at him in surprise—he had forgotten that only a few nights before he had been thrown into a rage at the suggestion that his own daughter might love this outcast—this brother of the beasts.

Ali-Es-Hadji could endure it no longer. With a cry he spurred his horse into the open, crying aloud to the man and the maid.

"Pig!" he shrieked, "take your vile hands off my daughter. Nakhla, come hither at once!"

But for answer there came the savage roar of a great lion, as the black-maned one leaped from his kill toward the advancing horseman.

Ali-Es-Hadji had forgotten the beasts in the moment of his rage, but now as he saw the fierce creature charging upon him he wheeled his horse and raced off in the opposite direction. Azîz at the same time leaped after the lion, crying to him to come back; and then the four stood together, the lion and the man with their mates, watching the intruders.

Again Ali-Es-Hadji rode within speaking distance, but this time his tone was less warlike. There was a note of pleading in it.

"Oh, Nakhla, my daughter," he cried. "Come back to me, my child. Do not leave your old father, who loves you, to die in loneliness of a broken heart."

It was Azîz who answered.

"Ali-Es-Hadji," he said, "I shall wed your daughter; and we shall come and dwell in your douar, if you will, that you may have her near you. I have no anger against the father of Nakhla."

"Come," said Ali-Es-Hadji—"it shall be as you have said."

With the lions snarling savagely at either side of them, Nakhla and Azîz walked forward to meet the girl's father. His terrified mount snorted and reared. It was impossible to bring him close to the wild beasts. Neither could Colonel Vivier approach without dismounting; and as there was none to hold their frightened horses the two men were compelled to ride on in advance of the four, for Azîz would not send his companions away.

Thus the strange party came to the camp of the soldiers and the Arabs, and very near they were to starting a stampede as the lions passed the picket line.

Straight into the center of the camp they walked, while the French and the sons of the desert looked on in wide-eyed consternation. Azîz held his two beasts under perfect control, aside from a little savage roaring and growls of warning.

As the party halted before Vivier's tent, a sudden sharp pain shot thrugh the lion-man's aching head. With a low moan, he threw his hands above him and sank to the ground, unconscious. Nakhla was on her knees beside him in an instant; and the two lions turned questioningly toward his prostrate form, sniffing about him and brushing his cheek with their rough tongues.

For a few minutes they hovered restlessly about, growling viciously at the circle of men who dared not approach closer, though they paid no attention to the girl in whose lap their master's head was pillowed. The beasts were evidently suspicious and ill at ease. Again the male sniffed inquiringly at the supine body of the man. Then his muzzle brushed the cheek of the girl as with a low moan he turned away and strode majestically from the side of the man he evidently thought to be dead. Behind him, stealthy and sinuous, moved his great mate. Before them the ranks of the watchers opened with marvelous rapidity, until a broad line was formed through which moved the king and queen out into the night toward their wild realm. For a long time their cries could be heard, diminishing in the distance.

Immediately that they had departed, Colonel Vivier did what he could for Azîz. Toward morning the lion-man fell into a natural slumber, and then at last relief came to the suffering Nakhla, for she hoped that he would awaken well once more.

The clatter of the preparation for breaking camp aroused him. As he opened his eyes he saw Nakhla, sitting beside him looking down into his face. Behind her were Colonel Vivier and Sheik Ali-Es-Hadji.

Azîz came slowly to his feet. He saw those about him,

but beyond them he saw a wondrous vision. His head no longer hurt. His brain had never been more clear.

He saw a stateroom in a rolling ship. He saw a grey, old man burst in—his grizzled, upturned mustache bristling and warlike as his indomitable eagle eyes. He heard his words as distinctly as though no long years had intervened since they were spoken: "Quick, your Highness! Come on deck—there is no time to bother about clothes."

And beyond the ship, far, far away, he saw a stately pile of ancient masonry, set in a great park of linden trees and ash and oak. There were broad, formal gardens and great expanses of level sward. There were gleaming marble fountains throwing their shimmering waters into the warm sunlight. There were men in uniform standing guard—tall, spendid fellows. And there was a little boy who walked beside a sad-faced man, and when they passed the soldiers snapped their burnished pieces smartly in salute.

The Frenchman and the Arab and the girl stood watching the expression of the man's face. They knew that some great change had been wrought within him; but what, they could not guess.

At last he turned his eyes upon them. He saw the desert sheik and the descendant of the famous Count de Vivier of the reign of Louis XIV, and he smiled.

Nakhla took a step toward him. His eyes met hers. No longer was he a dog or a pig. Now he knew precisely what he was and what awaited his coming upon another continent if he chose to come.

For a long moment he gazed into the eyes of the girl, and then he raised her slim, brown hand to his lips.

"We shall be very happy in the douar of Sheik Ali-Es-Hadji, our father," he said.

TWENTY-FIVE

Magazines from civilization seep into many far corners of the world. One such, an illustrated weekly of international renown, found its way into the douar of an Arab sheik. The son-in-law of Ali-Es-Hadji was reading therein an account of the strange happenings in a far-off kingdom. He read of the assassination of King Ferdinand and Hilda de Groot, and he examined with interest their pictures and pictures of the palace and the palace gardens. There was a full page picture of General Count Sarnya, the new Dictator. There was also a picture of an elderly, scholarly looking man, named Andresy, who had been shot with many others by order of Sarnya, because they had attempted to launch a counter-revolution.

One day General Count Sarnya received a cablegram. It was from Sidi Bel Abbes. All it said was, "Congratulations! You have my sympathy," and it was signed, "Michael."

WHY WASTE
YOUR PRECIOUS
PENNIES ON GAS OR
YOUR VALUABLE
TIME ON LINE
AT THE BOOKSTORE?

We will send you, FREE, our 28 page cata-
logue, filled with a wide range of Ace
Science Fiction paperback titles—we've
got something for every reader's pleasure.

Here's your chance to add to your personal
library, with all the convenience of shopping by mail. There's no need to be without
a book to enjoy—request your *free* cata-
logue today.

 ACE SCIENCE FICTION
P.O. Box 400, Kirkwood, N.Y. 13795   A—05

ALL TWELVE TITLES AVAILABLE FROM ACE
$2.25 EACH

ANDRE NORTON